"Would you care to tell me about her?"

A lot of years had passed since Grandma last reached inside his heart in this way. He had almost forgotten her ability to see through a person.

"I was thinking about Kate Long," he admitted reluctantly. His eyes traveled around the warm, cozy kitchen before refocusing on Grandma's wrinkled face. "She's a very stubborn, independent person."

Grandma's eyes sparkled as she smiled. "A little like you, Son."

He shrugged. "I don't see the likeness myself."

Grandma laughed and laid a hand over his. "I don't imagine you would. I did notice the moonstruck glances you were casting her way during church, though."

" 'Moonstruck glances'? Absolutely not!" he said. "Why, I don't even like—"

JENNIFER ANN RYAN is married with two teenage children. Her dad and four siblings and their families all farm Australian land near her. She plays the piano and keyboard, knits complicated sweaters, and sews some of her own clothes, but her all-time favorite hobby is reading. "I've been hooked on it since I first tried to copy the words from my brother's schoolbook at age four." She is fortunate to write full-time. *Good Things Come* is her first published novel.

Good Things Come

Jennifer Ann Ryan

Heartsong Presents

For Mum and Jean.

A note from the author:

I love to hear from my readers! You may correspond with me by writing:

Jennifer Ann Ryan
Author Relations
PO Box 719
Uhrichsville, OH 44683

ISBN 1-58660-204-7

GOOD THINGS COME

Cover illustration by Jocelyne Bouchard.

PRINTED IN THE U.S.A.

one

The child hurtled toward him, a pink and blue blur of movement that materialized into sturdy arms, pumping legs, and flying blond hair. Aaron caught a glimpse of rosy cheeks before the youngster careened into his legs with the force of a miniature freight train.

"Oomph!"

He had no choice but to swing her up into his arms. A pair of laughing blue gray eyes met his.

"Whoops!"

Her face broke into an engaging grin as she surveyed the world of the small parking lot from her elevated height. "What's your name, Mister?"

His eyes searched the area for a parent or guardian. He shifted the child onto one hip and gave a mock salute. "My name is Aaron Frazer."

The child giggled and placed a small, trusting hand against his cheek. "Hello. I'm Suzie. I'm almost four."

At the emphasis, Aaron grinned and wondered just how long it really was until her fourth birthday. "Almost, huh?"

An anxious voice called the child's name then, and she turned around. "Uh-oh. Mama's coming."

Aaron followed the child's gaze. A slim woman darted through the crowd toward them, a plastic carrier bag clutched in one hand. She wore navy slacks and a fluffy white sweater. Where the child's hair curled, the woman's fell straight to her shoulders and framed her pale face in a honey-blond curtain. Her brow puckered in a worried frown.

"Suzie!"

Relief crossed her features, quickly replaced by an implacable expression as she drew near, her gaze locking on Aaron. The slightly wide mouth firmed; the thin straight nose flared briefly and stilled. Only the blue gray eyes so like her daughter's remained alive, as her gaze darted from Aaron's face to Suzie's and back again.

"I'm sorry," she said. "I hope my daughter hasn't given you any trouble." She tucked some loose strands of hair behind her ear. "I've told her never to run off without me, but she's at an adventurous age. I don't think she understands the dangers."

Aaron lowered the girl to the ground and stretched out his hand toward the mother. "She was no trouble. I'm Aaron Frazer."

The woman placed her small hand hesitantly in his. "Kate Long."

He could see tension in her eyes and in the set of her shoulders—and something lonely about her. Even here in the Saturday afternoon shopping crowd, she had a solitary air, like a single tree growing from the rocks on a mountainside.

Suddenly Aaron wanted to open his arms to her, to provide a safe haven. It was an odd way to feel toward a stranger. A compelling desire to know this woman filled him.

She looked down at her daughter. "Suzanne, you mustn't run off like that. I could have lost you, and I've told you not to talk to strangers."

The little girl hung her head. "Sorry, Mama. I forgot."

While Kate Long gave an exasperated shake of her head,

Aaron took a step forward. He caught a hint of violets mingled with the smell of fresh bread, pastry, and coffee that characterized the mall. The floral scent suited her.

When Kate spoke again, her eyes met his. For a brief, telling second, he saw her interest reflected there; then she looked away.

"Thank you for minding her," she said. "Now I really must go."

He glanced at her bare fingers and then at her face again. "Your daughter is a sweet little girl. Don't blame her too much for running off. All that energy has to go somewhere."

"Yes." Kate's gaze shifted behind him to his Harley road cruiser standing nearby, strayed back to his jacket and blue jeans, and snapped away again. Something shut down in her face.

She backed up a step, tugging the child with her. "I hope she won't do this again."

"No harm done," Aaron assured her. "I guess you're new here? A move for the whole family?"

She scooped her daughter into her arms. "There are only the two of us," she said without expression.

"Then allow me to welcome you to Ferntree Heights, Kate." Aaron enjoyed the sound of her name as it rolled off his tongue. "If you wanted to live in the prettiest part of Australia's Blue Mountains, you've found it."

As he spoke, a kookaburra flew into the lemon-scented gum beyond them and burst into joyous, laughing song.

Yes, the mountain range west of Sydney was a special place. Aaron looked off to hazy mountain peaks in the distance. The smell of pine trees and gums, the crispness of the air, the winding roads and occasional winter snow, all meshed together into the place he called home. He thanked God every day for his life here.

Kate kept her eyes averted as she spoke again. "I want Suzie to grow up here among the mountains where the air is clean and she can feel close to God."

"That's an admirable desire," he offered quietly, wondering at the wistfulness in her voice.

"Thank you," she said, dropping her gaze.

He could see in the shadow of her eyes that she wanted to leave. "I shouldn't keep you out in this cold any longer," he said. "It was a pleasure meeting you and Suzie."

Kate nodded. A flicker of relief crossed her face. "Good-bye then."

"Not 'good-bye,' " he said. "I feel certain we'll meet again soon."

❦

The next morning Aaron sat beside his grandmother in church and wondered what had happened to him when he met Kate Long. A man accustomed to feeling in control, he didn't like the powerless feeling of letting his thoughts constantly stray in her direction.

Now she sat almost parallel to him in the small A-frame church, half hidden by the broad-shouldered form of the town's elderly plumber, her slumbering daughter cradled in her arms.

The sun shone through the stained-glass window at her back and gave her an almost ethereal quality. Her golden hair glowed around her head.

When the service ended, Aaron stood and gave his navy jacket a tug. "If you'll excuse me, Grandma? I'll phone or drop by this afternoon. I see someone I want to speak to."

He stepped away from his elderly relative and quickly followed mother and daughter to the exit. "Kate!"

Her body stiffened before she turned to face him, with a glance toward the door.

"I hope you don't plan to leave already." Aaron couldn't mistake her reluctance to speak with him, but he wasn't about to be put off. He ignored the slighted feeling her near snub gave him and glanced around. "I'm sure there are a lot of people who'd like to meet you. Stay and let me introduce you to some of them."

Kate looked at him as she moved the child slightly in her arms. "Not today." She glanced down at her slumbering daughter. "I really must go."

"I'll drive you home then."

At her raised eyebrows, he laughed softly. "Not on the bike," he said. "I have the truck today."

"Oh." She paused and eyed the exit again. "I can manage on my own. I don't have far to go, and I've left the baby stroller by the door. Besides, weren't you with someone?"

"My grandmother has her own car." Aaron caught Kate's look and held it. "It's cold outside. If you're worried about coming with me, a dozen people here will vouch for me."

After a pause, Kate wrinkled her nose and sighed. "You're right about the cold. Thank you. I'll accept the lift."

❦

Kate slipped the drowsy Suzie into the backseat of Aaron Frazer's crew cab. She disliked allowing even this small inroad into her independence, but her daughter didn't deserve to travel home cold when a perfectly sensible alternative had been offered.

"Hey, Honey." She smiled and tweaked her daughter's

nose. "You had a little nap. Mr. Frazer has kindly offered to drive us home."

"I'm sorry her sleep has been disturbed," Aaron said. "I hope this won't mess up her routine."

"It's okay." Kate slid into the front seat and watched Aaron circle to the driver's side of the vehicle.

Since David's death she had worked hard to build a new life for herself and her daughter, a happy life for just the two of them. She would always respect God in her heart and wanted to teach her daughter that respect too. But since she felt He had ignored her cries for help when she most needed it, she didn't plan to lean on anyone but herself ever again. Not God and not another man.

Something about Aaron Frazer—she couldn't explain what—made her feel that her plans would not be easy to follow. She didn't like that.

"What's your address?" he asked into the silence.

For an embarrassing moment Kate's mind remained blank. Then she remembered the new details. "Forty-one Hollie Avenue. It's not far from the mall."

"Yes, I know it," he said. "A block of four apartments, red brick, right on the corner."

Surprised, she nodded. "That's right."

He laughed. "It's a small town. You'll soon know it just as well as the locals do."

As Aaron started the truck and eased out onto the road, Kate noticed a pile of brightly colored leaflets on the floor of the vehicle.

Aaron followed her gaze and nodded at the leaflets. "I own a fencing business," he said. "The crew cab is great for times when I have the whole team working on a single job. We can go together and still store our equipment in the tray space at the back."

Curious in spite of herself, Kate looked at him. "What kind of fences do you build?"

"Whatever people want," he replied. "Most of the work I do is basic fences, corrugated color-bond sheets, wooden palings, and chain mesh, but what I love most is to work with wrought iron. I don't get the chance to do much of that."

While he talked, Kate studied his face. It was a sturdy face, not handsome, but open and reliable. He looked and sounded successful. "You must enjoy your work."

"I do." Ending the short drive, he signaled the turn and pulled into the space in front of her apartment. "Here we are."

Kate unbuckled her seat belt and reached for the door handle. "Thank you. I appreciate the ride."

Aaron climbed out, retrieved Suzie's stroller from the backseat, and helped the child down. "It was a pleasure."

When he turned to her, Kate offered a hand and a formal smile. "Thanks again."

He grasped her hand firmly. "I'll carry the stroller to the door for you."

She shook her head and withdrew from the slight contact. "No, really, you've done enough by offering us a lift." She picked up the stroller herself and took a step backward.

For a moment his brows drew together, but then he smiled. "It was my pleasure."

She nodded.

"I'd like to see you again," he said abruptly.

Heart fluttering uncomfortably, she spoke. "I plan to attend services each week at Saint Luke's."

At her attempt to brush him off, his enigmatic smile flashed out. "I'll look forward to seeing you again."

Not certain whether she should be relieved or concerned by his words, Kate nodded. "Good-bye."

❦

The next day Kate donned her most businesslike dress. After nursing her ailing Volkswagen on the journey to Ferntree Heights, she had taken the car to the mechanic's shop. It was now doubly important that she find work quickly.

A picture of Aaron Frazer popped into her mind. She would like to carry his aura of confidence into her interview at the employment agency.

Her teeth clenched. That man had found his way into her thoughts far too much, and such imaginings owned no place in her life, not anymore. She had learned the hard way that the things you put your trust in can fall apart in an instant. She simply must not make herself vulnerable again.

Yet she had enjoyed seeing him yesterday.

"Oh, stop it, Kate!" she chided herself.

"Mama?" Suzie looked at her curiously.

Kate glanced at her daughter, the joy of her life and the single good thing to remain from her marriage. It was hard to believe she would be four in just a few short months. "Nothing, Darling. Mummy was just thinking out loud."

There were no other clients when Kate arrived at the employment agency. She gave her name to the receptionist and sat on one of the gray vinyl chairs beside a large potted plant. Apart from the scratch of the receptionist's pen as she worked, the only sounds came from behind closed doors. The muted tap of fingers on a computer keyboard, the occasional rustle of paper.

After a brief wait, a door opened, and a dark-haired woman stepped out. "Kate Long?"

Kate nodded and stood. "Yes."

"I'm Marie Baxter. Please come this way."

As Kate followed, the woman led them into a spacious office and settled Suzie in a corner with some toys. She was a refreshing change from the busy, disinterested workers Kate had met at other agencies.

"Won't you sit down?" Marie stepped behind the desk, and her smile deepened. "I recognize you from church, although we didn't get a chance to meet yesterday. My brother drove you home, I think."

At the casual linking of her name to Aaron Frazer's, Kate cringed. "Yes, but I barely know him. We happened to meet at the mall the day before. . . ." She looked into Marie's kind brown eyes and trailed off.

"Well, I'm glad to have the chance to meet you," Marie said emphatically. "When we've concluded our business, I hope you'll accept an invitation to come to my home this evening for dinner. My husband is overseas, and it would be a relief to have some adult company and conversation."

The woman possessed an inherent friendliness that was impossible to ignore.

Despite her inclination to protect herself from possible hurt by remaining distant, Kate's cautious heart warmed to her. "Thank you. That's very kind."

Marie smiled and waved a hand. "It's nothing really. It will be a great pleasure for me, I assure you." She straightened in her chair. "Now how can I help you today?"

Kate pushed her resumé across the desk. "I'm looking for work. Part of the reason I decided to move here was because I was told by one of the metropolitan employment agencies that the job prospects are good, especially for people with secretarial skills. I can manage up to twenty hours a week. I have a current driver's license, but my car is in the shop." She met Marie's gaze frankly. Normally she would keep the details of her situation to herself, but in this instance she was prepared to make an exception. "I don't plan to get it out until I have solid work and can save some money toward it, but I realize lack of transportation may rule out some positions. If so, I may need to rethink my cash-flow priorities. I also need recommendations for reliable daycare providers."

"Oh, dear." Marie glanced over some papers on her desk and then up at Kate. "I'm afraid whoever told you job prospects were good here must not have known that Carter's Chickens has closed down. Some seasonal jobs are available during the summer months, but right now things are rather tight. Carter's provided employment for over two hundred people. When they closed, many of those two hundred people wanted other jobs. I have over fifty names on my books from Carter's alone, and most of the jobs I had vacant closed very quickly once they started looking for new work."

Kate's heart sank. She had been so certain that Ferntree Heights would be right for her and Suzie. She had paid out bond money on the apartment and would have a large car bill too. She simply couldn't afford to pack up and relocate. "Please tell me of anything at all that you have. I'll work anywhere that's ethical and within my abilities."

When Kate left the agency an hour later, she shook her

head. In her hand she held a list of three job possibilities, all local, and the only ones Marie could offer that were remotely suitable. She also had details of one reliable babysitter and definite plans to have dinner at Marie's home that evening.

Kate listened with a frown to the bouncing sound of the stroller as she negotiated the hilly sidewalk back to the apartment. This wasn't the start she had anticipated.

It might be nice to form a casual friendship with Marie Baxter, she thought, *but nothing too close.* She pushed aside the image of Aaron Frazer that continued to encroach on her thoughts. A friendship with his sister would be a much safer choice!

❦

Kate visited Marie again the following week. As they were talking, Marie, without Kate's prompting her, told her guest the nature of her husband's absence.

"Jeremy is on a tour of a number of Third World countries," she said quietly, "where he'll install and demonstrate the use of a water purification product his company markets."

"It must be difficult," Kate murmured, "trying to cope without him."

Marie nodded, her lips tightening as she collected their empty coffee cups from the table and stepped to the sink. "His job doesn't usually take him away from home," she explained. "When this opportunity came up, he seemed eager to take it. I'm concerned about his health and safety in some of the areas where there's political unrest. And, yes, it is difficult to cope on my own with three children."

Kate knew what it felt like to worry over an absent

husband, although in a very different way. Her heart softened toward the other woman. "Do you hear from him? Can he let you know how he's getting along?"

"Jeremy contacts us whenever he can." Marie sighed as she rinsed the cups.

Marie had her back turned, but Kate could hear the unease in her voice when she spoke again.

"It isn't really that," Marie said finally. "I keep wondering if Jeremy cares whether he's here with us or not."

She turned to face Kate and shrugged her shoulders. "Would you listen to me? He'll be home in a few more months, and I'm probably just being silly."

Relieved that Marie didn't want to confide further, Kate glanced around the all-white modern kitchen as Marie refilled their cups. She would comfort Marie if she could, but what could she say? Her own experience had convinced her that sometimes there was no comfort.

"Shall I tell you about my week?" she asked instead. "I have good news and bad news, as they say."

Marie smiled as she sat down again. "Please do tell me. The children are quiet right now, so we'll probably get a few more minutes of peace."

"I've added another talent to my long list of accomplishments," Kate said, smiling. "I can now package and label pottery articles for sale or shipment."

Marie laughed and raised her eyebrows. "So far so good. That will add a couple of lines to your résumé. What's the bad news?"

"After the first two days, my employer realized she hadn't really needed an assistant. She was simply a little behind with her orders."

Marie groaned. "She let you go?"

"Yes," Kate said. "I'd intended to come into the agency to tell you about it, but since you'd said you weren't very sure about this job, I knew you would contact me about other positions. I decided to tell you the next time we met."

Marie's face flushed with righteous indignation. "You know, I really don't like it when people do that. Your employer should have thought about whether she really needed an assistant before she came to me—"

Touched by Marie's concern, Kate laughed and held up a hand. "Don't worry about it. I'm sure there's a better job out there somewhere. Her studio was so cold that I had to put on about five layers of clothes, and the work was repetitive."

As they laughed, Kate glanced into the family room. A photo of Aaron stood on the old walnut piano.

"Gorgeous, isn't he?"

At the sound of Marie's voice, Kate started, but when she looked at her, she saw only sisterly pride in her expression.

Kate returned her attention to the photo. "You share his eyes," she murmured without thinking. "Not just the color—it's the expression in them, a kind of liquid warmth."

Marie laughed again. "Brown cow's eyes."

Kate shook her head without shifting her gaze from the photo. "Gentle eyes, and yet he is a very determined man."

Kate realized her thoughts had strayed dangerously and that Marie must be wondering at her sudden interest in her brother. She frowned at the photo. She hadn't meant to say anything like that at all.

Marie gave her a curious look. "Speaking of Aaron, I think that's him now."

Kate heard it, too, then—the unmistakable rumble of a powerful motorcycle as it approached the house. It echoed hollowly in the dense, cold weather. Her heart raced with a combination of anticipation and unease.

Since David's accident, she had never quashed her aversion to the big machines. She pushed the thought aside. The past was past.

When Marie's back door opened and closed, Kate glanced in that direction. Part of her was glad to see Aaron again, but the rest wanted to sweep Suzie away from her new playmates and escape.

Aaron removed his lamb's wool coat and stepped forward.

His sister rose to greet him, and he bore her affectionate hug good-naturedly. "What's up, Sis?"

He turned to Kate. "Nice to see you again, Kate."

Kate nodded and said the first thing that came to mind. "You're on that machine again."

He frowned. "Yes."

Kate lowered her head, appalled by her sudden rudeness.

"Is your daughter here with you?" Aaron asked after a moment. "How is she adjusting to life in Ferntree Heights?"

"Suzie is well, thank you," Kate replied primly, relieved that he had ignored her ungracious outburst, "and enjoying the new environment. She's playing in the back room with Marie's children."

"I'm glad you and Marie have become friends," Aaron said. "My sister has felt lonely for adult company."

"The company of a female is so much more entertaining than yours, dear brother," Marie teased, as she gave him another hug that belied her words.

Kate found it difficult not to envy the easy camaraderie

between the siblings. This kind of family interaction was something she had missed as a child. She was glad when Aaron put an end to the fooling around and became serious.

"Is there anything you need me to do for you?" he asked his sister.

Marie took a moment to think. "No, I don't believe there is. You've been looking after me so well in Jeremy's absence, there's really nothing. You spoil me, you know."

He laughed. "That's what big brothers are for."

While they continued the lighthearted chat, Kate searched for a way to end her visit.

Aaron preempted her. He gave his sister a quick peck on the cheek. "If you're sure you don't need me to do anything for you, I'll go. I'll come for a longer visit tomorrow afternoon, if you like."

With a brief nod in Kate's direction, he left.

Disturbed by the sudden plummet of her emotions, Kate stared uneasily at his retreating back.

two

Aaron noted the final measurement in the pocket notebook, rewound the measuring tape, and ran his hand along the worn timbers. As a child he must have climbed this fence a hundred times.

Now it needed to be replaced. He and Grandma Bennet had discussed it earlier in the week, and he'd promised her he would measure it today. If he hadn't already made the commitment, he would have stayed at Marie's longer.

He had seen Kate's prickliness when he arrived at his sister's house. She clearly felt uncomfortable in his presence, but Aaron had decided the first day he saw her to get to know her better. A man accustomed to action, he had regretted leaving so abruptly.

"She's been married and has lost her husband," he muttered to himself. "I guess that would make a lot of women cautious about getting to know another man. I'll have to find a way past that."

"Do you have all the figures you need, Son?" his grandmother called from her porch.

He tucked the notebook in his shirt pocket, crossed to the porch, and stepped up to smile at his diminutive relative. "I sure do. I'll be ready to start work in a couple of days."

"Good, good." She waved an arm behind her. "Come along inside now and have something to eat. The Lord has blown a frosty breath on us today."

Aaron tossed down the measuring tape, removed his work boots and coat, and followed her inside. "The Lord blows frost on us every day this time of year, Grandma," he pointed out wryly. "It's hard to believe Sydney is just over the mountains, yet so much warmer."

She nodded. "You have to remember that they're on the coast, and although we're not far away topographically, we're up in the mountains."

"A geography lesson, Grandma?" he asked with a smile.

She gave him a playful swat to punish his teasing.

His smile remained in place as he followed her into the kitchen. The smell of freshly baked pie tickled his cold nose. "Mm, hm! Are you sure you don't want to come live with me?"

She gave a ready laugh. "I'm glad you enjoy my cooking. I find the kitchen a soothing place."

"Given the amount of time you spend here, you should be as large as a house," he teased. "I know why you're not, though. You give most of what you make away—or force it onto your poor, unsuspecting relatives."

He fell silent suddenly. A vision of Kate Long in his kitchen danced through his mind. Would she wear one of those old-fashioned frilly aprons? Or was she a more modern cook? Maybe she didn't cook much at all.

His grandmother broke into his reverie quietly. "You're far away, Son, and I suspect I know why. Would you like to tell me about her?"

Her voice jolted him back to the present. He glanced at the piece of pie before him and took a sip of the hot coffee.

"Excuse me, Grandma?" he asked, hedging.

"The young lady you visualized in your kitchen," the old

lady said shrewdly. "Would you care to tell me about her?"

A lot of years had passed since Grandma last reached inside his heart in this way. He had almost forgotten her ability to see through a person.

"I was thinking about Kate Long," he admitted reluctantly. His eyes traveled around the warm, cozy kitchen before refocusing on Grandma's wrinkled face. "She's a very stubborn, independent person."

Grandma's eyes sparkled as she smiled. "A little like you, Son."

He shrugged. "I don't see the likeness myself."

Grandma laughed and laid a hand over his. "I don't imagine you would. I did notice the moonstruck glances you were casting her way during church, though."

" 'Moonstruck glances'? Absolutely not!" he said. "Why, I don't even like—"

Grandma held up an admonishing hand. "Of course you do, and there is nothing at all to say you shouldn't. From what I've seen of her, she's a delightful young woman, and her presence in church would suggest she's interested in God and His people."

"Perhaps," he conceded, "although something she said made me wonder if she likes to control her own life too much to trust the Lord."

Grandma ran a hand over the tabletop. "Perhaps she hasn't learned yet to lean on Him."

Aaron shrugged. "Maybe. She certainly doesn't appear to like me. She has some attitude about bikes or bikers—or something."

Grandma stayed silent a long time before she spoke again. "I don't know about the motorcycles, but if you have serious feelings about this woman," she held up a hand as he started to protest, "and you believe those feelings are of the Lord, you'll have to show Kate Long just how much there is to like about you."

She paused to pat his hand. "That is, if you think she's worth the effort. Maybe it's just a passing curiosity on your part." She said it in a dismissive tone and began to gather the dishes they had used.

"She's a fine woman," Aaron said sharply. "More than worthy of any man's interest." His brows drew together. "You might not know she's struggled alone since her husband died and has provided single-handedly for her daughter while she worked all kinds of jobs to make ends meet."

He hadn't known it himself, until his sister raised the subject on the phone one evening.

Brown eyes met brown, and he realized how revealing his defense of Kate Long had been.

He shook his head. "Why do I feel as if I've just told you my deepest secrets?"

His grandmother gave his hand a final squeeze. "I didn't mean to upset you," she said. "It's important that a man knows what he really wants when it comes to matters of the heart. Sometimes that takes a little prod from someone else." She gave him a thoughtful look. "My boy, I suspect if you want to pursue your interest in Kate Long, you may have a bumpy road ahead of you. That child has experienced some troubles. I see it in her eyes. A man would need to be patient with a woman like her."

Patience wasn't exactly his strongest trait; in fact, it was one he had always had difficulty with, but Aaron guessed there was a first time for everything. "Not that I'm saying

I'm interested," he said cautiously, "but if I was interested in Kate Long and she didn't return the feeling?"

His grandmother shook her head. "I don't know, but perhaps the Lord has given her a place in your heart for some special reason," she offered. "You may discover, though, that she just needs to find her way."

❦

A grin tugged at Aaron's mouth as he stopped the truck outside Kate's apartment a month later. Slowly and surely he had worked to gain her trust until she now seemed at ease with him. With winter upon them, he no longer rode the motorcycle. Since she didn't appear to like the big machines, he thought that could have worked in his favor too.

Kate's friendship with his sister had allowed him to see her with pleasing regularity, and now she had accepted his offer of a lift to the annual church talent night. He felt quite proud of his steady progress.

Aaron glanced down at his clothes. Tan trousers, off-white shirt, and dark brown sweater. The padded green jacket looked okay but didn't really match. He frowned at his sudden obsession with his appearance.

"You look fine," he muttered crossly as he climbed out of the vehicle. "Stop acting like a nervous adolescent!"

By the time he reached the apartment, Kate had ushered Suzie outside and shut the door, which firmly squashed any idea he might have had of seeing the interior.

He blew on his cold hands and allowed his gaze to move over Kate's face until it settled squarely on her clear eyes. "Hi."

"Hello." Her breath huffed around her face in steamy

clouds. She stepped forward, somewhat impeded by her daughter, who clung to her legs.

He nodded at the child with raised eyebrows. "What's wrong with her?"

"Nothing," Kate said. "She's just feeling a little shy tonight."

A peculiar sensation squeezed his heart. He bent toward the child. "You haven't told her I eat almost-four-year-old little girls for breakfast, have you?" he asked.

A tiny giggle erupted, and Suzie glanced up.

Aaron found himself staring into smiling eyes that looked so much like her mother's that they took his breath away.

"Hey, don't you look lovely tonight?" he told the little girl. "What's that on the front of your sweater? I see something peeking out from under your coat."

As she stepped forward to display the butterfly motif, Suzie's shyness disappeared. Wondering at the sudden tenderness welling inside him, Aaron admired her clothing before ushering mother and daughter into the truck.

During the short drive, he kept up a stream of nonsensical banter with Kate's daughter. He couldn't help noticing that her mother remained silent.

"Here we are." He stopped the truck in a parking space outside the church facility and walked around the front to help Kate out.

For once she didn't fight him but laid her hand on his arm to step down. Their eyes met. Hers were full of sparkling anticipation before she quickly shielded them with lowered lashes.

Tonight she wore thick navy blue pants with a lighter blue sweater. A hip-length blue wool coat completed the outfit. Her eyes reflected the colors she wore.

"You look very nice," he said quietly. "I didn't really have a chance to say so earlier."

He heard the catch of her breath and felt her hand freeze on his arm before she stepped to the ground. Pleasure sparkled in her eyes for a moment before she looked down.

"Thank you," she murmured.

"You're welcome," he said with a nod.

He turned abruptly to open the rear door of the crew cab. "Out you come, Suzanne Long."

When he had unfastened Suzie's seat belt, the child crossed the seat and threw herself into his arms with a giggle.

Kate spoke from behind him. "Tonight's shyness was quite out of character. Usually it's 'Aaron this' and 'Aaron that.' "

He liked it that his name came up between them. Still holding the child, he turned and held out his free arm to Kate. "Let's go inside."

Children's artwork adorned the walls of the church's multipurpose room. The exposed beams of the ceiling were festooned with streamers. A sense of excitement hung in the air. Aaron quickly slid Suzie to her feet and helped Kate shrug out of her coat, then removed his own. They sat in the row of chairs already occupied by his sister and her children.

Feeling like a frog in a fish bowl as he sensed the curious eyes of many of the congregation upon them, Aaron kissed Marie's cheek. "Hi, Sis. Hi, troops."

When Kate finished settling Suzie, he did his best to ignore the interest they were attracting and leaned back so that Kate and Marie could chat.

It was a mistake.

Now Kate's hair fanned across his shoulder. His hand itched to reach up and touch the fine strands. Would it feel as soft as it looked?

He was saved from further contemplation when the pastor cleared his throat through a microphone and announced the beginning of the talent night.

In the first act the youth group performed a rather hilarious Battle of Jericho. At the first sound of Kate's laughter, a ripple of pleasure engulfed Aaron.

Later they played games. As they caught their breath at the end of a set of egg-and-spoon races, Aaron smiled at Kate.

Suzie sat high on his shoulders like a little monkey. Her squeals of delight blended with the noise and laughter.

"This is what I wanted for her," Kate said over the din. "I'm so glad I found her a loving church family."

We could make our own family, Kate.

The thought took Aaron by surprise. He had been so proud of his patience that he had allowed his feelings to deepen undetected. He was startled to discover he suddenly wanted everything. As he tried to absorb this information, someone bumped into them.

Aaron couldn't stop the forward impetus that almost knocked Kate off her feet. Her hands came up to grip his arms, and for a moment they teetered as they searched for balance.

Then the three of them—Aaron, Suzie and Kate—were locked in a kind of triangular embrace, with Suzie half held by each adult. Words from a recent wedding ceremony he had attended played through Aaron's mind.

And so the triangle is completed, husband and wife joined to each other by the loving embrace of God.

Their small triangle reminded him a little of that concept. Without conscious thought, he dropped a kiss on Kate's nose. His free hand stroked through the strands of her hair. The contact ended in seconds, camouflaged by the melee going on around them.

While Kate stood motionless, he eased Suzie out of her grip and lowered her to her feet.

When their eyes met again, Kate's reflected her wariness. "What was that for?" she whispered.

He shrugged, uncertain of the best way to answer.

Suzie wrapped her arm around his leg. He glanced down into eyes grown wide with awe.

"You kissed my mama," she whispered.

Aaron struggled between a frown and a grin. He had kissed Kate and enjoyed it too!

The grin won. "Yes, I did," he said.

At the close of the evening, he shepherded his guests into his truck and started toward their apartment. Suzie fell asleep almost the moment she sat down, and a silence settled over the vehicle.

When the ride ended, Aaron turned to Kate. "Did I embarrass you back there? I'd hate to think I spoiled your evening."

Her hair covered her cheek as she glanced downward. "You didn't spoil it." She hesitated, then turned until they faced each other. "Really, it's okay."

"You're sure?" he asked.

She nodded.

He lifted out the stroller and placed it beside the apartment door while she carried her sleeping daughter. "Do you have the key?"

Silently she handed it over.

He opened the door and leaned forward to slip the stroller inside the darkened room. "Good night, Kate."

"Good night." She stepped inside, flicked the light switch, and closed the door.

❦

Kate checked the hood of Suzie's waterproof jacket to be sure it was tied firmly in place. The first snow had fallen yesterday, leaving a chill wind in its wake.

She pushed the stroller the last few meters over the cobbled path to the bank. Three rounded marble steps led to a set of double oak doors, and she turned to lift the stroller up the steps. Moments later a blast of warm air met her as the door opened from within.

Aaron's familiar voice fell on her cold ears. "Let me help with that."

The moment they had cleared the door, Kate turned and stepped away, putting the space of the stroller between them.

She recognized the interest in Aaron's eyes and decided there was only one way to make her position clear. She squared her shoulders. "I'm glad we've met. I'd like to talk to you if you can spare a couple of minutes."

"All right." He gestured across the road to a coffee shop. "I'll meet you at Maggie's when you finish your business here."

She nodded. She would have preferred to air her thoughts outside, but she must consider Suzie. It wouldn't be fair to keep her out in the cold unnecessarily. "I'll meet you there in a few minutes."

The visit to the bank did nothing to improve Kate's frame of mind. She had enough money left to pay a month's rent and to buy food if she spent wisely. After that, she would be forced to dip into the savings she had so carefully hoarded for Suzie's education.

Where was God's plan for her good that He promised in the Bible? Why couldn't she feel His comforting presence?

She shot a glance heavenward. *I know I haven't been praying much lately, but if You're listening, if You care at all, please help me find a job before this money runs out.*

She carefully tucked the bank notes into her purse, maneuvered the stroller down the stairs, and headed for the cafe, Aaron, and what she expected would be an unpleasant confrontation.

From inside the coffee shop, Aaron listened to the muted chink of silverware on fine bone china as he watched Kate cross the road. She looked like a highly padded pixie in her thick brown winter jacket. He amended the thought. She looked like an *adorable* highly padded pixie.

As she wheeled the stroller through the automatic doors, he rose from his seat. Once Kate and her daughter were settled, the waitress appeared. Aaron smiled and turned to Kate.

"What would you like?" he asked her. "Croissants, cinnamon toast, a caffe latte, or cappuccino?"

"Nothing to eat, thanks." Her hair bounced around her face when she shook her head.

Was she thinner than the last time he had seen her and too proud to accept even the offer of a pastry from him?

She hadn't found another job yet. It frustrated him that he couldn't take care of her financial needs for her. He had been praying for her every day, but God was certainly taking His time to answer!

Kate smiled at the waitress. "Could I have a Vienna coffee, please?"

Aaron refrained from pushing Kate to eat something, ordered a caffe latte for himself and warm milk for Suzie, and folded his hands on the table.

When the drinks arrived, Kate met his look with a direct, implacable glance.

"There is something you have to understand," she began, "but first—" She squared her shoulders. "I appreciate your great kindness to Suzie and me since we moved here. In fact, you were really the first person to reach out to us, and I'll never forget that."

Aaron took a sip of his latte. "It was nothing."

She clasped her hands on the table. "I'm not interested in starting a relationship with you," she said bluntly. "If I've given you any impression other than that, I want to apologize." She took another sip of coffee, glancing away and then back. "That may not have been your intention anyway, but I need to make sure you understand—"

He drew a deep breath and exhaled slowly. "I apologize if my attention has caused offense—"

She leaned forward, a grieved look on her face. "I'm sorry. I just don't want—I can't—"

"You don't like me?" he prompted. "Is that what you're trying to say?"

"No!" She lowered her voice. "No, that isn't it. You're a very nice man. I do like you, and in other circumstances I would like your friendship. But I'm just not sure I can handle it right now. I know I can't if you always want more from me—"

He covered her hands with one of his. "Look at me, please, Kate."

She slowly lifted her gaze to his, her blue gray eyes turbulent.

"You've been open about this, so I'll do the same. I'm starting to believe God may have a plan for the two of us," he said. "I don't know what it is, and maybe it's just wishful thinking on my part. But I think you're beginning to believe it too. If He does want us to get to know each other better, I believe you'll find a sense of rightness in your heart about it. I think you should at least allow for the possibility."

three

Aaron watched his sister's agitated movement as she fidgeted with the handle of Grandma's old-fashioned teapot.

Now that Marie had related a little of Kate's troubles, she had his undivided attention.

"How long does she have before she has to move out?" he asked.

Marie ceased fidgeting with the teapot and looked at him. "Kate has ten days to find somewhere else to stay," she said flatly.

A whole range of feelings rushed through Aaron—concern for Kate, disappointment that she had chosen to confide in Marie when she refused even to acknowledge the possibility that he may have a place in her life, anger that she would be turned out of her home. He pushed the rest of his pumpkin scone aside.

Marie continued to explain. "I told Kate that I'd help her look around for another apartment tomorrow. I'm pretty sure, though, that she doesn't have enough money to cover the costs of getting into a new place. We haven't discussed her finances intimately, but her car is still at the mechanic's. I think she would get it out if she had the funds."

At the thought of Kate struggling that way, Aaron clenched his jaw. What was taking God so long to answer his prayers for her? He had wanted to help Kate the day they met at the cafe, and now he wanted to even more. To see her struggling while he had plenty went against everything within him.

"I'll pay the mechanic to do the work," he declared, "and I'll send Kate some money anonymously. She need never know who gave it."

Grandma shook her head as she removed the teapot from where Marie's agitated fingers had found it again. "Kate would guess that the gift came from one of you. She wouldn't expect anyone else to know of her financial position."

Aaron released a frustrated growl. "The Lord doesn't give us material blessings just for our own benefit. What's the use of having money if you can't give to someone else's need?"

"I already told her she could stay with us if she can't find somewhere else," Marie pointed out. "I wouldn't let her suffer, but you have to remember there are other places she can turn to with this kind of problem." She folded her arms. "I think Kate would probably be more comfortable with that than if you tried to give her funds."

Aaron frowned at his sister but dropped the matter of the money. Marie was right. Independent Kate would prefer to get help from a professional organization. That was the cause of part of his irritation. He wanted to help her.

"Your place is too crowded," he told Marie. "Where would they sleep?"

Marie's brows drew together in a frown. "It's better than sleeping on a park bench."

"I simply wanted to point out the difficulties." Aaron rubbed the top of his ear. "She can stay at my place then."

Marie shot him an exasperated look. "Where would you go?"

"I could sleep at the workshop," he said.

Marie laughed. "I can see that would work."

In truth he would probably freeze to death the first night. Aaron didn't normally have trouble thinking sensibly, but today he could focus on only two things: Kate's problem and his desire to fix it for her. "Then I'll come and stay with you," he told his sister.

Marie threw her hands up in the air. "You just told me I don't have room for anyone else!"

"When I said that, I meant Kate and Suzie," he snapped. "I can sleep on the floor."

They glared at each other until their grandmother started to laugh.

Aaron swiveled his gaze to her lined face. His frustration boiled over. "I don't find the situation amusing," he told her. "Kate could be homeless if we don't do something."

For a moment they all sat in silence. Aaron's frustration quickly gave way to shame.

"I'm sorry, Grandma." He took her hand. "I didn't mean to speak to you that way. I just feel so steamed up and helpless. She won't even talk to me when I see her these days. How can I get her to let me help her?"

He saw Marie's mouth form an "O" of surprise and fixed his sister with a glare. "Don't say a word."

She shook her head. "I won't."

Grandma laid her hand over his. "I have an idea, but have you asked the Lord what He thinks is best?" she asked quietly.

Aaron realized he should have taken the time to pray about Kate's dilemma, instead of arguing with Marie. Then perhaps he would have known the right way to go, instead of releasing his frustration by scrapping with his sister and being rude to his grandmother.

Forgive me, Lord. Your word says that You make all things beautiful in Your time. Help me be patient as I wait to see that promise fulfilled in Kate's life.

He shot Marie an apologetic glance and turned back to his grandmother. "What do you have in mind?" he asked her.

The old woman's clear eyes gleamed with anticipation. "I've been lonely lately. As people age, they become more frail, you know." She lifted one of her hands as if to emphasize the point.

Aaron had seen that same hand set hammer to nail, weed the garden, knead bread, and even mow the lawn on occasion. Most of these recently!

"I could be starting to lose my memory," his grandmother continued. "Last week I couldn't find my reading glasses, and there they were right on top of my head."

Aaron frowned. She had been doing that for as long as he could remember. "You've never shown a sign of frailty in your life," he said flatly.

His grandmother went on as though he hadn't spoken. "Sometimes elderly folk are too proud to ask for help," she explained, "but that doesn't mean they don't need it, and you know the Lord works in mysterious ways." Here she stopped and gave Aaron a pointed look. "Perhaps if someone were to speak to Kate about me, explain that I've been lonely, she could find it in her heart to move in here for a time to keep me company."

Aaron glanced at his sister, and it was their turn to laugh. Finally he looked back at his grandmother. "Do you mean this?"

She nodded vigorously. "Of course I do. I have been lonely and wondering what to do about it. Lately this old house seems too large for one. There's nothing I'd like more than to have Kate and her daughter stay with me. It would be like having a young family again, and perhaps in some way it will turn out to be a blessing for all of us."

❦

Kate glanced at the copper-plated wall clock and climbed the stairs of the apartment to the small bedroom she shared with Suzie. Marie would be here in a few minutes to help her search for a new apartment. How she disliked the lack of independence not having her own car caused her!

"Suzie, it's almost time for us to leave," she said. She appreciated Marie's generosity but hated to put her friend out.

Suzie lay sprawled across her bed, playing with her favorite bear. "Hi, Mama."

Kate smiled and lifted the little girl into her arms. "I see you've been having fun with Teddy. Let's go downstairs now and find you a snack before we have to leave."

Suzie's arms tightened around her neck as they descended the stairs. "I'm Aaron's Miss Mouse. I like Aaron."

"I know you do, Darling," Kate said. "You tell me so about a hundred times a day," she added under her breath.

Suzie stared solemnly into her eyes.

Kate dropped a kiss on Suzie's head and slid her to the floor of the kitchenette. "Let's get that snack."

Ever since Aaron had suggested it, Kate couldn't quite get the idea out of her mind that maybe God did have a plan for the two of them. She had begun her daily devotional times again and felt closer to the Lord than she had since before David's death. In His presence she was finding the comfort she needed, but she wasn't sure she was ready to consider a future outside the one she had so carefully planned. The truth was, she didn't know what she wanted. Since their discussion, Aaron hadn't pressured her. She should have felt relieved. Instead she found herself wishing he would treat her as he had before their talk.

She handed her daughter a box of sultanas and rubbed her temples where she could feel a headache building. "You can bring your snack along. I think I just heard a car pull up outside."

Kate opened the door to peer out and stared in surprise at the red crew cab parked at the curb. As she hovered in the apartment doorway, Aaron climbed out and strode over. Snow clung to his hair and shoulders.

"Hi, Kate."

"Hello," she said cautiously. "What are you doing here?"

"I know you expected Marie, but I've come instead." He paused and ran his hand over his hair to dislodge the clinging flakes. "Could we go inside for a moment? I need to talk to you."

Kate opened the door wider and stood back. "Of course. Come in."

As Aaron stepped inside, Kate paused to open the drapes to their full width. The snow outside the window continued to fall in thick flakes.

"You've made a nice home here." Aaron indicated the room with the swing of one arm. "The dried wildflower arrangements are pretty. Is that Everlasting Daisy?"

"Yes," she said, a glow of pleasure warming her face. His praise meant more to her than it probably should have. "Thank you."

"Aaron, Aaron!"

Kate's daughter launched herself at their visitor and squealed and giggled when he swung her up into his arms.

"Hi, Miss Mouse," he said.

While Aaron listened to Suzie's chatter, Kate put the kettle on. Suzie had never bemoaned the lack of a daddy, but soon she would be old enough to start asking questions. Kate didn't want her daughter to try to substitute Aaron for her lost father. The child would be too hurt when nothing came of it.

She placed a steaming cup of coffee in front of Aaron. "This will warm you. It's very cold out there."

Aaron stared at the drink with a startled look. "Thank you."

Kate groaned inwardly. She had been trying to keep her distance, and yet she had memorized how he liked his coffee and made it for him without even asking.

She gestured for Aaron to take the sofa while she sat on a chair. When he had given Suzie a final tickle and set her down, Kate pulled her daughter close.

"Would you like to play upstairs for a little while, Darling?" she asked gently. "Aaron and I want to talk."

Suzie nodded. "Okay, Mama."

Kate turned to him when her daughter left, laughed a little nervously, and fingered the scalloped edge of her china cup. "She's growing up so fast."

"She's cute." Aaron's smile was distracted. "Kate," he said determinedly, "I came here to see you today because I want you and Suzie to move in with my grandmother."

"Why?" Kate immediately drew into herself. If this was about charity, if he was asking because he knew of her financial difficulties—

Aaron hesitated over his answer just long enough to cause Kate concern.

She set her cup down and leaned forward. "Is Mrs. Bennet all right? She's not sick?"

Aaron shook his head. "She's—feeling well enough."

"Then what is it?" Kate asked. "I won't accept—"

Aaron held up a hand. "Grandma is lonely. She told me so herself. With you out of work, it only makes sense—"

"No." Kate stood and moved to the window. The sky withheld its burden of snow for the moment. Speech came easier with her back to him. "I can't move in with her. It was a kind thought, but—"

Aaron's words fell into the silence. "It would ease our minds if someone could be there to keep an eye on Grandma. I've never heard her talk about getting old before, about loneliness or becoming forgetful."

Kate's first instinct was to refuse again, but she took the time to consider his unexpected proposition. While she hated the thought of charity and recognized the dangers of accepting a home with a relative of Aaron's, if Mrs. Bennet really was lonely, it could be the answer to her prayers. She had wanted to believe God cared about her needs. Maybe this was proof that He did. The matter at least warranted further discussion.

She turned and met Aaron's gaze. "Is this what your grandmother feels? Or does she want to help me because she knows I need a place to stay? Did you or Marie put her up to it?"

He lowered his drink and looked at her. "She believes the Lord wants you and Suzie to live with her for awhile. That's all I can tell you."

He stood up and stepped over to the coat stand. "I hope you'll at least consider her offer." He smiled wryly. "I can call back later when you've had time to think about this."

Kate realized with surprise that she didn't want him to leave. She closed her eyes for a moment in silent prayer. What should she do? The Lord said He would provide for all her needs. It would be wrong to throw that provision away if this was His way of helping her.

She crossed the room to face Aaron. "There's no need to do that. I can give you a decision right now."

"What is it?"

Kate spoke before her courage and conviction could desert her. "I'd like to accept Grandma Bennet's kind offer."

The words were out, and she felt a surge of relief that made her certain she had done the right thing. Maybe the Lord cared more than she'd thought. Maybe He hadn't deserted her in her last time of need. Maybe He had been there all the time, but in her fear and sense of failure, she hadn't recognized His presence.

If moving in with Aaron's grandmother meant she saw more of Aaron, Kate told herself, aware that would be the major difficulty in the relocation, she would find a way to deal with that.

Aaron's eyes reflected his pleasure. "I'm glad you made the sensible choice." He rubbed his hands together. "Where would you like to start with the packing?"

Kate held up a hand. "Are you sure your grandmother will want us so soon? I thought we'd stay here until we had to leave."

"She wants you, believe me." Aaron hesitated. "On second thought, it would be best if one of us gets the utilities disconnected and notifies the agent you intend to leave today. With your authorization I can do that while you pack and then—" He broke off midsentence.

Kate could almost see the backpedaling motion as he realized he had tried to take charge of what was essentially her responsibility. She should have been irritated, but instead she found the vulnerability oddly endearing.

"That is," he amended a little sheepishly, "I hope you can use my help." The corners of his eyes crinkled. "I didn't mean to give you the steamroller treatment."

Kate watched as he straightened the collar of his coat. "I don't have much to pack," she said. "If you can see to the details downtown while I begin, I'd appreciate it."

It didn't take Kate long. Armed with the empty boxes she had used last time and stored flat in the space beneath the stairs, she packed, labeled, and taped the boxes quickly.

Suzie jumped up and down, full of excitement, but Kate couldn't berate her. She felt rather excited herself.

When Aaron returned, they loaded everything into the truck, delivered the apartment key to the real estate agent, and made their way across town to Mrs. Bennet's house.

Kate felt Aaron's eyes on her and turned toward him. "Are you sure your grandmother will want us straight away?" she asked again.

Aaron shot her a quick, reassuring glance. "I'm absolutely sure. You'll see for yourself when we get there."

Kate did.

The welcome shone from Grandma Bennet's dancing eyes as she met them almost before the truck drew to a standstill.

The older woman clasped Kate's hands. "My dear, I'm so glad to have you. Come in. We'll do a tour of the place while Aaron starts on those boxes. It's a good thing the snow has let up."

She bent to whisper something into Suzie's ear. Whatever secret they shared made the child's eyelids pop open. Suzie skipped along beside Aaron's grandmother, chattering away as though she had known her all her life.

They explored the rambling brick and fibro home slowly, stopping occasionally for Grandma Bennet to answer one of Suzie's endless questions. The spacious kitchen yielded golden buttery Anzac cookies and a glass of milk, which Suzie consumed eagerly.

When they returned to the living room, Aaron had several boxes stacked neatly in a corner.

"Where shall I put it all, Grandma?" he asked.

"Will it suit you to store what you don't need in one of the spare rooms for now?" Mrs. Bennet asked Kate. "We can take the rest of it to the bedrooms for you and Suzie."

Kate nodded. "That sounds fine, but I have a box of groceries that can go to the kitchen."

The front door opened, and Marie and her children spilled into the living room. "I'm glad you phoned me, Grandma. We wouldn't have missed this." She hugged Kate, then her brother. "What's first?"

As the day wore on, Kate's optimism climbed. Grandma Bennet's welcome seemed so genuine that she felt completely wanted.

Hope built in her heart as she soaked up the loving atmosphere that filled every corner of the rambling old home. She placed the last of Suzie's clothing in the antique dresser. "That's everything, I think."

Marie tossed the last empty box out through the open door while Suzie fussed over the coverlet of her new bed.

"Hey!" a masculine voice growled.

At the sound of Marie's stifled laugh, Kate turned. Aaron stood in the doorway, the box covering his head.

"Look what you did to me." His muffled voice came through the cardboard as he nodded his head wildly. "Somebody help me."

Suzie broke into giggles. "You're just 'tending."

"Are you sure about that?" Aaron bumbled around and pretended to walk into one of the walls.

Kate's heart swelled as he entertained her daughter with his antics.

"Suzie, why don't you help Aaron get the box off his head?" She gave her daughter an encouraging smile. "I'm sure he'll bend down for you to do it."

When Suzie removed the box, Aaron lifted her into his arms and carried her, giggling and chattering, down the stairs.

With Marie beside her, Kate followed.

"I do hope your grandmother doesn't mind all this activity." Kate paused and smiled. "What I'm trying to ask is, will the noise be a problem?"

Marie's laugh sounded warm and comfortable. "She'll thrive on it."

When evening came, they gathered around the big dining table off the living room. Silence fell as Grandma Bennet seated herself.

The old lady folded her hands and bowed her head. "Dear Lord, thank You for Kate and Suzie. May Your blessing rest on them as we welcome them into this home. Please use this food to fuel our bodies and strengthen us for tomorrow's service to You. Amen."

Kate swallowed against the sudden lump in her throat. Much time had passed since she had felt God's loving presence so keenly. She had a feeling that here in this home she would find her way back to Him.

She glanced at where Aaron sat flanked by his two nephews and felt her heart melt. He was another problem entirely, and she didn't know what to do about him!

four

A week passed before the next snowfall. Kate tucked Suzie's feet into the bright yellow waterproof boots and tied the hood of her jacket. "All ready?"

The little girl hopped from one foot to the other. "Yes, yes, yes!"

Kate laughed. "Okay, Honey, let's do it."

The pair raced outside into the snowy playground of Grandma Bennet's backyard.

Suzie giggled her pleasure as she scooped up handfuls of snow. "Look at me, Grandma! Look at me! I'm going to make a snowman."

"Are you sure you're warm enough, Grandma?" Kate asked Mrs. Bennet as she joined them in the yard. She felt a glorious sense of belonging each time she used the form of address the older lady had requested.

"I'm just fine, Kate. I may be short, but I have enough meat on my bones to keep the cold out. I wouldn't miss the opportunity to watch this precious child enjoy God's wonderland for the world. We haven't had this much snow for a long, long time. Let's enjoy it while it lasts."

For the next hour they scooped up mounds of snow to fashion Suzie's first snowman, complete with carrot nose and eyes and mouth made of small stones gathered from the garden.

Afterward they moved inside to the warm kitchen. Kate

gave Suzie a quick snack and ushered her to the living room and her toy corner. "Play awhile, Suzie, please, while I talk with Grandma."

Once Kate and Grandma Bennet were settled in the kitchen with steaming mugs of coffee, Kate faced the older woman with determination. She'd had her suspicions since her first day here, but now she had confirmed them.

"Grandma," she began sternly, "there's something we need to talk about—"

The older lady studied her serious face and uncharacteristically broke in before Kate could finish.

"I can't believe all that snow outside, can you?" Grandma Bennet fussed with her coffee cup, looking downward. "We've already had more than we normally get in a whole season. We may even set a record this year."

Kate refused to be distracted by the obvious ploy to change the subject. "You're about as frail as your hearty grandson, Grandma," she declared, "if you'll excuse me for saying so. I think it's time we acknowledge that both of you schemed to get me here."

For a moment surprise registered on Grandma's face. Then she began to laugh. "Oh, Kate, you do know how to get straight to the point. You are good for my old heart." She gave her hair an absent pat and became serious again. "First of all, if we're going to be fair, Marie was there that day, too, not just Aaron and me."

Kate felt her mouth twitch up at the corners, but she managed to straighten it out again. "Since Suzie and I came here, you've lost your reading glasses twice. That's the only evidence of forgetfulness I've seen, and your social calendar would rival that of a woman half your age. I doubt that loneliness is a problem you battle often either. I don't think you needed me at all."

Her amusement faded. "I feel like an imposter. It's wonderful to be here with you, but I have so little to give in return. Are you sure you want us, that we're not inconveniencing you?"

A wrinkled hand reached out to cover hers. "You've given beyond what you could imagine, my dear. It's true that we all discussed your situation. We were concerned because we care about you. I didn't ask Aaron to speak to you so I could drop a load of thoughtless interference on your head though. I really was lonely, and I really did believe it would please the Lord for the two of us to work together to meet each other's needs. Don't think for a moment that I haven't needed you, Kate. I have."

Her kind eyes sparkled with pleasure. "I've had more fun since you and Suzie moved in than I have had in a very long time. You've brought a breath of joy into my life at a time when many folks my age think only about death."

Kate turned her hand to give the old fingers a squeeze. "Thank you. That reassures me, and you've certainly made us welcome." She allowed a sigh to escape her lips. "Grandma, I'm very glad to be here, but I have had to admit that I don't understand why I've struggled so hard to find work. It seems every door I try is firmly closed against me. I'd started to believe God really was taking care of me."

Grandma Bennet nodded. "Sometimes it seems as if He isn't there, doesn't it? But I assure you He never leaves you or forsakes you. It's just that circumstances may make it difficult for us to see how He's working in our hearts and lives. Perhaps you'll find the Lord has a specific job in mind for you," Grandma suggested thoughtfully. "I'm sure something will come to light soon."

Kate smiled and stood to clear the dishes, her heart momentarily comforted. "I'm sure you're right, Grandma. I guess whatever job He has in mind for me will come along in His good time."

❦

At his office Aaron finished another customer record, saved the file, and shut down the computer. His office skills amounted to a medium level of enthusiasm, basic computer knowledge, and a two-finger typing style that did no more than get the job done. He felt much more at home on the work site than in the minuscule office of the warehouse suite. For that matter he'd rather be anywhere else inside the large converted shed that housed his supplies and samples.

He and his two workers divided their time so the office was always open for inquiries each morning. But he handled the paperwork alone, and lately it had been building up too much.

He glanced at the large pile that still remained on the desk, rolled his eyes heavenward in silent appeal, and hastily closed the door behind him. It was time to do the security check and get out of there, before he gave in to the temptation to tackle any more of it.

Sleet hit him in the face as he hurried toward the truck. "I hope Grandma's repair job is an inside one," he muttered.

At the thought of visiting his grandmother, he broke into a grin. She had found more reasons to get him there since Kate moved in than she had in the previous six months.

He turned the truck onto the road and laughed out loud. "Saves you from constantly trying to come up with excuses to spend time there."

He drove onto O'Reilly Street and pulled to a stop, still smiling. The weather may be chilly, but he had detected a thaw in Kate's attitude. The thought lightened his step as he climbed onto the porch and pressed the doorbell.

Kate answered the summons wrapped in one of Grandma's checked aprons, a smudge of flour on one cheek. Her surprise was obvious as she blushed prettily and buried her hands in the apron's pockets. "Aaron, hi."

"Hi, yourself." He dropped his gaze as he removed his boots.

Dressed in that cute way and so obviously happy, she took his breath away. Visions of the two of them together in their own home flashed across his consciousness.

The boots removed and his expression masked—he hoped—he looked at her. "I don't guess you've been mowing the lawn."

"Not in this weather." Her laugh was warm and infectious as she stepped back and gestured for him to come inside. "We're trying out a new recipe Grandma found in a magazine."

"Aaron, Aaron, you came!"

His mouth twitched as Kate lunged to stop her daughter from flinging her floury self at his legs.

"Yes, Miss Mouse, I came," he said. "Grandma has a job for me, I believe."

He met his grandmother's shrewd glance. "What needs to be done, Grandma?"

❦

Two hours later he wasn't so sure about his grandmother's matchmaking efforts. It was one thing to want to see Kate, entirely another to stand out in the sleet with his face so cold he couldn't feel it.

Not even the sight of the new fence he had built before Kate moved in could take his mind off the weather. Under the gloves his hands were almost numb. He hammered one last nail into the side of the wooden greenhouse, gathered up the rest of the tools, and headed back inside. He guessed the old saying about no gain without pain had proven itself today.

"All done." He stripped off his excess clothing and backed up to the large wood stove in the kitchen, conscious of Kate as she moved around the kitchen. Just being in the same room with her cheered him and made the memory of the hours spent outside fade. "It sure is cozy in here."

After lunch Suzie fell asleep on the sofa at his side. Each time he glanced down at the sleeping child or felt her hand stir where she'd laid it trustingly against his knee, Aaron experienced a rush of tenderness.

Did this paternal feeling have its rightful place in his heart? He was beginning to think it did.

"I've been wondering if you went to college before Suzie came along," he said to Kate presently. "You seem too young to have completed a course before then."

Kate sat forward, her face eager as she nodded. "I started an apparel manufacturing course. I completed only the first year." The smile dimmed. "I lost my grandmother during that year, and early the following year I married. As yet I haven't found a chance to go back and finish, but I'd like to one day." She smiled a little self-consciously. "I dream of creating my own line of apparel. I'd especially like to sew for children."

At this point Mrs. Bennet entered the conversation.

"Suzie's clothes are lovely."

Kate smiled. "Thank you. It's fun to create new ideas and see them come to life."

"It reminds us of everything the Lord has created," Grandma said, "including us! I think He must have felt the same sense of satisfaction we do, only on a much larger scale. Is that what you feel when you carve, Aaron?"

Aaron felt a twinge of discomfort as Kate looked at him.

"You carve?" she exclaimed. "As in wood carving?"

"Well, yes," he admitted. "I do a little from time to time." He met his grandmother's glance. "There's always a sense of satisfaction when the work is done, so, yes, I guess it does feel something like what the Lord must have felt when He created the world and everything in it, only in a much smaller way, as you said."

His grandmother stood and went to the dresser to retrieve one of her favorite pieces.

She handed the small box to Kate, who lifted it carefully to the light. He could almost feel the familiar design under his hands as she examined it.

"Why, Aaron," she exclaimed, "it's beautiful and so intricate. You must have spent hours on it."

Aaron released his held breath quietly. The need for Kate's approval took him by surprise. He hadn't realized he had been waiting for it. "You don't seem to notice the time when you're working," he said. "It's a soothing activity."

As her fingers caressed the carving, he decided to make a picture frame for Kate. He would carve wildflowers, mountain blooms, and greenery into its surface and then smooth the wood until it felt silken to touch. When finished, it would house a family portrait. Something that could hang over the mantle of his home to join with the special touches Kate would add to put her stamp on the place.

The thought felt right, so that he was able to accept it and the sense of responsibility that went with it.

"If I could ever get on top of the paperwork."

"Pardon?"

He realized he had spoken aloud and shrugged. "I spent all morning trying to catch up on my invoicing and records. I guess it's still on my mind."

As Aaron rose to leave later, Grandma asked Kate to see him to the door.

"My old bones don't want to leave this chair," Grandma said with a twinkle.

At the door Aaron waited quietly for a moment.

"I want to invite you to a Yulefest dinner this week," he said. "I don't know if you've ever attended one, but it's the closest Australia gets to celebrating a traditional Christmas in cold weather." He named a restaurant in nearby Katoomba. "Grandma or Marie would gladly take care of Suzie."

Kate gazed at him solemnly, and he found himself inwardly kicking again at all the waiting.

Frustration drove him to speak without thought.

"Well?" He snapped the word, determined to talk her into attending if she initially refused. "Do you want to come or not?"

"That would be nice," she surprised him by saying. "What evening did you have in mind?"

His eyebrows raised. He had all but dictated the words and was already regretting his impatience when he had recently prayed for the Lord to show him how to wait for her. He had expected a sharp putdown as fair reward for his bad manners. Her rapid acceptance left him wondering what to say next.

"You agree?"

Her laugh washed over him. "Don't look so shocked. I don't think it would be inappropriate for us to go along this once—as friends." She clasped her hands under her chin in a gesture that reminded him of Suzie. "I've never been to a Yulefest celebration, but I really would like the opportunity to celebrate the birth of Christ in a special way right now. I don't think I was quite as thankful as I should have been last Christmas."

As he drove home, Aaron tried to remember if he had sorted out the details properly. He must have, because Kate had seemed quite pleased.

At least one of them was happy. He let himself into his house feeling rather disgruntled.

It seemed that all he did these days was pray for help, take things back into his own hands, ask forgiveness, and do it all over again. Even now he found it hard to accept Kate's strictures on their outing.

Friends indeed.

He would have to do something about that impression!

Aaron made a harrumphing noise in the back of his throat. He would have to pray about Kate's attitude and wait for the Lord's direction. Surely if he kept reminding himself often enough, he would eventually learn the lesson and stick to it.

❦

As Kate dressed for the evening out, she decided she would offer to do some cooking for Aaron to return the kindness. He hung around Grandma Bennet's so much that it seemed clear the poor man lacked for decent home-cooked meals.

The chime of the doorbell and Suzie's shriek of delight left no doubt in Kate's mind that her escort had arrived. She smoothed the sky blue fabric of the high-collared dress, drew her coat over her arm, and left the room.

"Kate." Aaron's voice held a smile. "You look lovely."

The simple words engulfed her in a cocoon of happiness she couldn't seem to control. "Thank you."

She watched her daughter's eyes go wide. "Oooh, Mama, aren't you beautiful?" With girlish innocence Suzie turned to Aaron. "Don't you think so, Aaron?"

Aaron gave Kate a curious smile as he agreed. He helped Kate into her coat and shrugged into his own. Suzie's giggle wafted after them as they left.

As he helped her into the truck, Aaron glanced at Kate's shoes. "I hope you'll be warm enough in those."

Kate laughed. The Italian Sinso court shoes were a wonderful find from a pre-loved thrift store several years ago and the only "going out" shoes she owned. Not that she thought of them as "date" shoes, and in any case this certainly wasn't a date, she assured herself! Any occasion deserved her best shoes. "It was this or waterproof boots. We women have to be allowed a little vanity."

He shook his head. "Somehow I doubt you have a vain bone in your body. Your beauty is completely unaffected." He smiled. "I guess you're right though. Good old rubber boots wouldn't have quite done it."

Kate reminded herself again that this wasn't a real date. It sure felt like one, though, especially with Aaron paying her such kind attention.

A beautifully restored brick building housed the restaurant. Thick ivy trailed over the ornate latticework. A set of wide doors opened off the porch into a plush foyer. As they stepped inside, a stately gentleman greeted them and checked their reservation.

Kate glanced around as they walked to their table. Discreet bunches of holly adorned the door lintels, reflecting the Yulefest theme. Red and green silk ribbons decorated the centerpiece of gold candles on their table. On a dais at one end of the room, where everyone could enjoy it, stood a life-sized nativity scene with the Christ child at its center.

Kate had never been anywhere like this with David. Theirs had been a cheeseburger-and-fries kind of life on the rare occasions they ate out. She realized with a start that it didn't hurt anymore to think of those memories.

She turned to Aaron and smiled as they took their seats. "What a lovely restaurant, and the nativity scene is so life-like. Just looking at it reminds me of the wonderful gift we received that night long ago."

"I know exactly what you mean. It stirs your heart somehow, doesn't it?" He lifted the menu. "I'm glad we came, and I hope you'll find something here that you'd like to eat."

She smiled and ran a finger down the list of traditional Christmas fare. "It all looks so good that I'm not sure. What do you suggest?"

They settled on roast turkey with baked vegetables and cranberry sauce, followed by plum pudding. Aaron's quiet words of thanks to God before the meal touched Kate's heart again with a sense that this man was special and devoted to God.

Over the meal Kate did her best to draw Aaron out. She told herself she was only being polite, not hanging on his every word. "Tell me about the rest of your family. Marie says your parents are overseas at present?"

Aaron nodded, and she thought how handsome he looked as the soft lighting deepened the brown of his eyes.

"They did a house swap with a New Zealand couple," he explained. "I think since Dad retired, they're busier than ever."

"He was a judge, wasn't he?" Kate prompted.

Aaron smiled. "Yes. As children we never had a chance if we misbehaved. Dad always knew exactly how to get the truth out of us." He leaned forward, clearly enjoying the chance to talk about his family. "I have three younger sisters. Marie, you already know. She's the eldest. Debra is touring Europe with two of her girlfriends, and Phoebe, the baby, is studying to become a veterinarian. Debra visits whenever she can. Phoebe is the restless one. It wouldn't surprise me if she left Australia permanently once she has her degree. Debra, though, sees her trip now as a one-time experience. They both live in Sydney."

Kate smiled, intrigued by the diversity of his family. "They sound wonderful. I hope they don't henpeck you too much, the single male among three sisters?"

His deep chuckle washed over her. "I manage, although all of them from time to time decide I need a dose of mothering."

Kate watched his fingers as he toyed with his napkin. This giant of a man seemed far too self-sufficient to require female nurturing.

Yet my heart longs to take him in.

The thought took her by surprise. Unnerved, she quickly pushed it aside.

"What about you?" Aaron asked. "Are there no other relatives in your life? I can't imagine life without family. It would be so lonely."

The tone of his voice robbed the words of any suggestion of pity. She understood he must be curious about her past, but it wasn't something she would share. She could, however, tell him about her life now.

"I consider myself fortunate. I have a wonderful daughter, I'm settled where I want to be, and I've made good friends. The only lack I have is in finding work, and I've been trying to trust God with that need."

Time passed, and eventually she glanced at her watch and offered a reluctant smile. "I guess it's time we left. It's later than I'd realized."

His nod seemed to reflect her reluctance. "I expect Grandma will wait up so I guess we'd better head back."

In the truck he turned to her while the engine idled and the heater dispelled some of the chill. "I want to thank you for this evening. I enjoyed your company very much."

She fumbled with her seat belt, suddenly clumsy. "I enjoyed myself too. I hope I didn't numb you with all my talk."

His hand closed over hers where they still struggled with the clasp. "I wouldn't have changed anything about tonight, Kate. It was perfect."

He bent his head to clip the seat belt. Kate fought the urge to run her fingers through his hair. What was happening to her?

Sleet began to fall as they reached the house. Aaron

climbed from the truck and surprised Kate by lifting her into his arms before she could step down on her own.

She stiffened. "Put me down."

"Let me carry you," he said quietly, in much the same tone she imagined he might have spoken to his sisters when, as children, they wouldn't do quite what he thought was best for them.

"Your shoes would be ruined before you got to the porch," Aaron continued.

Kate realized it was true. Feeling a little silly for making a fuss, she allowed him to carry her. "All right, but just to the porch."

Aaron followed her instructions to the letter. Then he lowered her slowly to her feet on the porch, his eyes gazing deeply into hers.

She knew, then, that he was going to kiss her. Part of her warned her to step back and break the tenuous moment, but something stronger, hidden deep within her heart, kept her still.

He bent his head and for a moment stared into her eyes. Then he touched his lips to hers.

It didn't matter that their lips were cold or that sleet dampened their faces. Her heart lifted at the featherlight movement that offered so much tenderness. She searched his face and found sweet, soft warmth there. It radiated from his eyes and lifted the corners of the lips that had brushed hers.

His eyes reflected the sense of wonder she knew must be in her own expression.

"That shouldn't have happened," Kate blurted as she reminded herself, much too late, of the danger of getting too close to this man.

As Aaron remained silent, she stumbled on, babbling to cover her awkwardness. "I'd like to repay you for this evening's invitation. I hope you'll let Suzie and me do some baking for you this weekend."

For a long moment they stood in silence, Aaron's gaze searching her face intently.

"Getting close to you is about as easy as trying to push a car up a mountainside," Aaron finally murmured. He took some deep breaths before he spoke again. "I'm sure you're a fine cook, Kate, but I don't want you to pay me back with baked goods. That's not what tonight was about."

She moved a step closer to the door, farther away from him and closer to denial of what had just happened between them.

"We went out together as friends," she insisted. "I thought I could repay the favor by baking for you. I don't have a lot else I can offer—"

He pushed a hand through his hair. "This evening was much more than a couple of hours in the same room together, Kate, and you know it. I kissed you just now, and you kissed me back. That wasn't a friendly gesture. It was something to be given between a man and a woman who have special feelings for one another."

She started to shake her head but stopped as she met his gaze. "I told you—it was a mistake. I should never—"

He stepped forward. "Don't take away from what we shared. It was special for both of us. Be honest enough to admit that."

He stood there waiting, fists buried deep in his trouser pockets.

She ached to return to the comfort of his arms, longed for the security and acceptance she knew she would find there, but she shook her head. "I can't. I told you—"

"There's something between us," he said, his voice uneven as his hands gripped her elbows. "You won't be able to pretend it out of existence forever."

She raised troubled eyes to his. "Aaron—"

He waited. "What is it?"

"I'm afraid of what you make me feel," she admitted. "It's too much. I can't control it."

"It scares me too," he murmured, "sometimes. I guess we have to place ourselves in His hands and trust Him to take care of us and lead us in the right direction, knowing He won't let us come to harm."

five

Kate looked up from staring at the rose pattern of Mrs. Bennet's gray and blush living room carpet, to the piece of paper in her hand, and finally at Marie.

For almost two weeks she had tried to forget the kiss she had shared with Aaron on Grandma's front porch. For that amount of time she had faced the inevitable discomfort when they met, had tried without success to gauge his feelings toward her.

As winter showed the first signs of yielding to spring, her thoughts and emotions whirled like leaf debris caught in a brisk breeze.

She stared at the folded paper again.

The irritating little note.

Her blood did a slow and, she assured herself, justified boil, until she wondered if a mirror would actually reveal steam shooting out of her ears.

In her hand she held a legitimate reason to feel frustrated with Aaron. She refused to consider that his apparent unconcern since that night might be the reason she wanted this confrontation.

No. This matter stood alone.

Aaron must think her a fool, unable to recognize a sham when she saw one. Worst of all, he must pity her, as though she were some needy object without any will or determination of her own.

She squashed the tiny voice that warned against misdirecting her anger, schooled her features, and met Marie's glance.

"This isn't a real job opportunity." She kept her voice carefully bland. Marie was the innocent party in this.

Marie toyed with the basket of pinecones by Grandma's fireplace. "Actually, Kate, it's really—"

Kate raised a hand. "No. You don't need to say another word. I understand completely, and I appreciate your position. If I were you, I'd have done the same thing."

After all, family ties were strong. Aaron and Marie would be no exception. Her quarrel wasn't with Marie, but with him. He needed to be set straight.

"So you're not upset? You understand that this is a great opportunity for you? You'll speak to Aaron about it? He's given you a head start by doing this," Marie said. "You get first pick at the position of his office assistant before I officially list it."

Oh, yes, she would speak to Aaron, Kate thought.

She avoided Marie's eyes. "I'll speak to him."

Marie gave a relieved sigh and bestowed a farewell hug. "I'm so glad to hear it. I hope it works out for you."

It certainly will work out, Kate told herself minutes later as she asked Grandma to mind Suzie. "I need to run an errand."

Grandma smiled and waved a hand in the general direction of the garage. "Why don't you take my car, Dear?"

"I'd planned on a taxi." Kate thought about driving the old BMW. She wouldn't have to pay the taxi to wait for her or try to anticipate when to ask the driver to return. It would make it easier for her. "If you're sure, Grandma—

that would be a real help."

While she made the short drive to Aaron's house, Kate's annoyance grew. When Marie had shown her Aaron's handwritten advertisement for someone to handle the paperwork for his business, it had taken her by surprise. When she realized he must have created the job because he felt sorry for her, she felt hurt and angry. These feelings were fueled further by a lingering frustration that she was still out of work. She felt as though God had abandoned her again, and she resented Aaron's apparent indifference to what had passed between them.

Wearily, she pushed the confusing jumble of thoughts aside and focused on the note. She might not be able to do much about the rest of it, but this did not represent a real job opportunity, and she certainly didn't intend to become the subject of Aaron Frazer's pity.

The paper made a crackling sound as her hand clenched it to the steering wheel.

"It's a good thing Grandma could mind Suzie," Kate muttered upon arrival at Aaron's house. "I wouldn't want my daughter's tender ears to be singed when I tell Aaron what I think of what he's done."

She stopped herself from fingering the wrought-iron gate Aaron had handcrafted as she pushed it open. Ignoring the early flowering rhododendron shrubs that flanked each side, Kate marched up the path. The brass knocker begged for a firm hand. She enjoyed the chance to deliver not one, but several resounding clangs to announce herself.

The door opened inward, and Aaron's face appeared.

"Kate, what a nice surprise." He paused as he registered her expression. Then he opened the door wide and waved an arm behind him. "Please, come in. What brings you to visit?"

Lost in his warmth, she almost forgot her purpose. Then she recalled what she gripped so tightly in her hand, and the resentment surged back. "There's something I need to discuss with you."

He gave her a puzzled glance. "Sure."

He ushered her inside and led her into a spacious sitting room where a wood fire crackled. Plum throw rugs enhanced the polished board floor. Kate noticed several carved wood animals on a shelf in one corner but reminded herself she was in no mood to appreciate his craftsmanship. The fat little wombat sure was cute, though.

Kate turned determinedly away from the decorations and refocused her glare on Aaron.

He pushed his hands into the pockets of his navy sweats and gave her a somewhat mystified glance.

"What is it?" he asked. "You seem—disturbed."

She shoved the paper in front of him. "Don't pretend not to know why I'm here. I know exactly what you've been up to."

His puzzled frown looked so convincing that she thought he should have chosen an acting career.

"I'm afraid I don't know what you mean." He motioned to one of the cane loungers. "Would you like to sit down?"

She eyed the floral lounger and, despite her determination not to notice, could see he had done a wonderful job of restoring the heritage-style home. She had always favored red brick homes, and this one seemed particularly welcoming.

"No, thank you," she said shortly, telling herself not to

think about those things. "I prefer to stand."

"Are you sure? You wouldn't like a drink? Coffee, tea?"

She shook her head. "No, thank you."

He raised one hand helplessly, frowned, ran it over the collar of his knit shirt, and dropped it back to his side.

He could stand there, looking sure of himself and pretending innocence, but Kate knew better. If he wouldn't acknowledge the matter, she would spell it out for him. She waved the paper under his nose. "Would you care to explain this?"

Startled brown eyes met hers for a brief moment as he caught the paper and her hand with it.

She drew away quickly. "Well?"

He finished reading and looked up at her. "Well, what?"

"That's a notice that you need an assistant to help out with office work at your warehouse suite," she said.

"That's right."

She resisted the urge to stamp her foot and balled one fist and placed it on her hip instead. "A part-time clerical assistant, grade two. Flexible hours."

She completed the quote she had memorized and stared her accusation at him.

When he didn't immediately respond, she took a step forward. "I am not a case for charity, Aaron, despite what you may think. I would have thought you'd have realized that by now. Frankly, if God doesn't want to help me, I'll help myself."

He tipped his head to one side. If she hadn't known better, she'd have thought a thread of hurt mingled with his apparent confusion.

A hot prickling at the backs of her eyes forced her to

turn her head away. She drew several deep breaths before she met his gaze again.

He twisted the paper into a thin strip between his hands. "I think there's been a misunderstanding here. If you'd let me explain—"

She lifted her hand quickly. "I don't think there's anything to explain. The situation seems perfectly clear. You concocted the idea of creating work for me. You knew I needed a job and chose this way to help me. While the thought is admirable, I do have some pride." She paused for breath. "Furthermore—"

"Hold on a moment, Kate, please."

The quietness of his voice silenced her. She looked at his face and felt surprise ripple through her.

A gleam of admiration crossed his face as he stepped closer. "I've never seen you this way," he murmured. "So alive and full of flashing fire and spirit. You are truly beautiful in every mood."

His words distracted her from the issue. She drew a sharp breath. "Stop that."

He gave an almost indiscernible shake of the head. "It's only the truth. I'm sorry you're upset, but I can't deny how your face glows. For the first time in my life I think I might have a clue as to why some men deliberately goad women. I had no idea someone could glow as you are now."

Shaken by this unveiled admiration, she ignored his statement and tried again to refocus on the purpose of her visit. "The position you've created is tailor-made for me, from the job requirements right down to the flexibility of hours."

He sighed and nodded. "I wasn't aware of the skills you'd acquired, but I imagined you had probably gained some clerical experience over past years, and I prayed hard before I—"

She shook her head in frustration. "You're not listening to me. It's clear you've made up the job, just for me. I can get a job on my own. I don't need you to find me a fictitious one out of pity."

He laid a hand on her arm. "I would never treat you as an object of pity, Kate, and I have every confidence that you can get work to support your daughter, just as you always have. But I wish you would let the Lord bear your burdens more."

She searched his eyes and found only sincerity.

Much of the anger seeped away, and she became aware of the warmth of his hand on her arm, of how close he stood.

For long moments she fought the urge to throw herself into his arms and hide there.

What draws me to this man, Lord? I'm sorry for my outburst. I want to trust You, but You know a relationship is not in my plans, and sometimes I don't see much of Your intervention in my life. Help me have faith.

She looked into Aaron's face, searching for an answer to this riddle. "Then why, what—?"

"I have a genuine part-time clerical position available," he said gently. "It's come about as the result of increased work. I no longer have the time to deal with all the paperwork. I wanted to give you first shot at it. Is that so terrible?"

Her heart plummeted as she realized how wrongly she had acted. Most of her anger had been misdirected anyway.

"This is a real job," she parroted in a dull monotone. She buried her face in her hands, as the way she had behaved replayed through her mind. "I'm so embarrassed. You may have offered me the very answer to my prayers, and I—"

He drew her hands down and lifted her chin to look into her eyes.

"I may run a successful business, Kate," he said quietly, "but I'm not in a position to create a job out of nowhere. If you think back, you'll recall I've mentioned times when I've spent many hours pushing paperwork over the weekends and in the evenings."

He stroked his hand over her cheek. "This is a genuine need. I don't deny I hoped I might also help you by hiring you if you were suitable, even hoped it might be the answer to your troubles. But I wouldn't have forced it on you." He dropped his hand and stepped back. "Any more than I would force. . .other things."

With her gaze fixed somewhere near the center of his broad chest, she replied, "I'm in the wrong. I don't know how to apologize. You must think I'm very immature and that I have no faith at all."

His arm came around her shoulder to hug her to him briefly as he led her to one of the chairs.

After they sat down, he spoke softly. "I think you're a very fine person who is used to making her own way in life. I admire you for that, but you must know that sometimes it's all right to accept help from others. If that weren't the case, how would any of us ever share the good things God has given us?"

"That's true, I suppose," she admitted, staring at the floor.

He unfolded the paper and smoothed it. One finger tapped the print. "Will you apply for the job?"

She glanced up at him. "I'm not sure you should still want me to. I've burst into your home and accused you wrongly." She could feel her cheeks burning. "I'm so sorry."

He waved a dismissive hand. "Consider it forgotten. Now will you apply for the job?"

The job was tailor-made for her. It would provide money for Suzie's education fund and for daily living. Eventually she would be able to have the car repaired. If a stranger offered the same terms, she would jump at them.

Foolish pride didn't belong in this situation.

"I'd like to, yes."

"Great. Then let's talk about what the job entails."

When they had finished their discussion, she climbed into Mrs. Bennet's car, returned Aaron's wave, and drove away slowly. She felt stunned, a bit overwhelmed, cautious, and exhilarated. Despite the embarrassing display of misplaced irritation, she had landed herself a job.

Yes, but what have I gotten myself into by taking this job? she wondered.

"Today has enough worries," she reminded herself, "so relax. This is a wonderful job opportunity, the open door I've waited for." She smiled and patted the car's dashboard. "We'll let the rest of it worry about itself, right, Car?"

❦

The red truck slowed to a stop outside Mrs. Bennet's front gate. Kate quelled the flutter of nerves in her stomach, kissed her daughter good-bye, and strode purposefully through the chilly morning mist toward Aaron and her new job.

I can do this.

"Is Suzie okay about staying with Grandma?" Aaron

asked as she climbed into the truck.

Kate fastened her seat belt and nodded. "You don't think it will be too much for your grandmother, do you? When I told her about the job, she really wanted to care for Suzie. The sitter I used before is no longer available, but I could have arranged for her to attend a daycare."

Aaron glanced at her before he pulled onto the road. "Frankly, I think Grandma will love it. Spending time with children makes her feel young again."

Kate relaxed a little. "That's what I thought too."

Aaron drove into the Ferntree Heights industrial area, past a truck depot and a paper recycling plant. Sheds with brick-fronted façades flanked either side of the road. They seemed to mock Kate's bravado.

She had never worked in a warehouse suite. When Aaron turned the truck into the lot, a shiver of disquiet ran down her spine.

The rumble of motorcycle engines issued from the foremost shop section of the warehouse. A group of leather-clad riders clustered by the door. Several of them stared at the truck as it passed. One raised a gloved hand.

Aaron waved back.

A moment later he searched her face, and she tried to look confident.

"You have—" she began, clearing her throat against the telling squeak. "I see you have a motorcycle, uh, group next door."

He pulled the truck into a vacant space and turned toward her. "Also a screen printing service and a camping equipment outlet."

He stepped out, waited for her to close her door behind

her, and locked the truck. "Warm enough?"

Kate started. "I'm fine."

"I know it's your first day at a new job," Aaron said, "but there's no need to be nervous."

He led her to the door of Frazer's Fencing. "This is it. I'll give you a quick tour and then show you what you'll be working on today."

As the morning progressed, Kate became more and more uncomfortable. In the small confines of the office, she knew her jumpiness stood out.

About midmorning, Aaron stood and pushed his hands into his pockets. "I think you know enough now to continue with those invoices. If any customers come in, find out what they want, take down their details, and tell them I'll get back to them this afternoon."

"You're leaving?" She couldn't ask him to stay, but she would have preferred to have his company.

He nodded. "I should check on the guys, see how their job is progressing. You have my cell phone number if you have any questions."

"All right. Will you be back before I leave? I don't mind walking home—"

He took a step toward her. "I'll be back in time to drive you. Wait for me."

"Thank you. I guess I'll see you later then."

Kate was thankful for his willingness to drive her home. The prospect of making her way past all those rumbling machines and leather-clad strangers made her feel like half-set pudding.

She knew it showed weakness on her part to want him there, but Kate wished Aaron hadn't decided to leave. She did her best to blot out the rumblings, mutterings, and occasional shouts from next door, and eventually she succeeded.

So well, in fact, that when Aaron returned and she noticed him looming in the doorway, she jumped.

"You startled me." A rush of warmth stole into her cold cheeks. "Is it that late already?"

Disturbed by the firm clench of his jaw, she glanced away on the pretext of checking her watch. "My goodness, it is. I'll just take a minute to close down the computer and straighten the desk. I'm sorry. I should have been ready."

"There's no need to apologize." He almost growled the words, crossing to the other side of the room. "When you finish, wait in the truck. I'll set the burglar alarm and lock the door."

Aaron climbed into the truck, turned the key, and gunned the engine. He glanced at her out of the corner of his eyes. She scrunched against her door, her mouth a straight line.

He had hoped that if they spent more time together, it would help their friendship along. Instead he had felt compelled to leave the office because she seemed disturbed with him so near. He had spent several hours outside getting under his workers' feet, only to come back to a Kate so uncomfortable with him that the mere sound of his voice unnerved her.

So much for the gentle progress he had believed God was bringing about. This patience thing was a big waste of time!

He eased the truck into gear and focused on the road. "How did everything go after I left?"

"I got through more than half of the invoices that were on the desk," Kate said.

"That's great." He changed gears for a corner. "You did much more than I'd have managed in that amount of time. Were there many calls?"

"No." Her laugh sounded hollow. "A couple of people phoned to discuss options. I took down their names and numbers and a brief outline of their questions. It's all on the desk for you."

He nodded. "I'll phone them after I drop you home. Business declines some over winter. A lot of folks don't start thinking fences until the weather warms. Did anyone stop in?"

"No. I only had phone calls."

Too soon they arrived at Grandma's. Aaron knew he could follow Kate inside, have a hot drink, and spend some time, but he wouldn't.

Kate had made it pretty clear to him that she didn't want him around.

Lord, where are the answers to my prayers? I waited on You, and for awhile I thought things were going somewhere. But I could have fenced the entire state of New South Wales in chain mesh by now, and I still haven't earned even a bit of Kate's affection.

He turned in his seat to face her. "I'll see you tomorrow morning."

Her fingers plucked at the seat belt after she took it off. "Aaron, I—"

"Is something troubling you? If it's about working for me—"

She shook her head quickly. "No! Work is fine. I'm sure I'll get settled. The first day is always the hardest." She tilted her chin into the air. "I won't let you down. I promise."

"Is something else on your mind then?" he prompted.

"No, it was nothing important. Just—thanks for giving me the chance." She opened the door, stepped down, and turned back to face him. "I'll see you tomorrow. Thanks for the lift."

six

Three weeks passed. Three weeks in which Kate discovered that driving to work with Aaron wasn't as easy as she had thought it would be. The constant closeness made it hard for her to maintain her emotional distance from him.

So she did some calculations, visited the bank, and organized to get her car back on the road.

As she drove away from the mechanic's shop, Kate's hands caressed the familiar old steering wheel. She had transportation again!

"Our first stop will be the mall," she decided.

Suzie clapped her hands. "Our car! Our car! Yip-de-yodel-do!"

Kate laughed. "That it is, Honey. God has blessed us with not only a job for your mama and a lovely place to stay, but this as well. I'm very thankful."

She drove the car into an empty space near where Aaron had stood with her daughter that first day. He had looked so right as he held Suzie in his arms.

She quickly purchased the ingredients on her list and returned to Mrs. Bennet's. Yes, Aaron had looked right that day, but she wished she didn't think so. To travel that road would only hold heartache for her and her daughter. She knew because she had walked it once already and carried the scars to prove it.

She took Suzie inside and locked the door behind them.

"Hi, Grandma. We're back. Is it okay if I use the kitchen for awhile?"

Mrs. Bennet's eyes twinkled. "Of course, Dear."

An hour later Kate sat behind the wheel of the car again. The smell of cinnamon and apple muffins permeated the air. She ignored the memory that she had offered to cook for Aaron once before and been firmly rebuffed.

This was different. She owed him some form of thanks, and she was determined to give it to him. It would also be a way for her to let him know she was independent again and no longer needed his help.

"I'll look a bit silly if he's not even there," she muttered as she nosed the vehicle into Kookaburra Drive.

"He's there, Mama," Suzie insisted with the optimism of the very young.

Indeed, several lights shone out into the dull day from the front windows of Aaron's house.

Kate checked her reflection in the rearview mirror, tweaked the collar of the teal blouse into place, and inhaled slowly. "Okay, Suzie, let's give Aaron our gift."

Suzie bounced up and down on the seat as she waited for Kate to help her out. "A present for Aaron! Oh, goody!"

Kate didn't plan to enjoy this occasion. It was to serve as a reminder to both her and Aaron that she intended to maintain control of her own life. She felt a little nervous as she lowered the knocker.

The door swung open, revealing Aaron's smiling face, his surprise and pleasure at their visit apparent. Oh, if only she could see inside this man and know what he was thinking.

Kate mentally shook her head. This from the woman who mere seconds ago had been telling herself the importance of keeping her distance!

"Look what Mama made!" Suzie exclaimed before either spoke.

Kate gave a wry grin as she handed over the covered platter of muffins. There was nothing like having your efforts trumpeted far and wide. "It's partly a celebratory gift, partly to say thanks."

"That's very nice of you." Aaron bent to sniff the rich aroma. "Please come inside." Swinging the door wide, he stepped back to make room for them to enter. "What are we celebrating?"

Kate couldn't help smiling. "I'll give you a clue. It has roof racks and is burnt orange, old, and recently out of the repair shop."

He raised his eyebrows. "You got your car out? That's great."

Somehow she found herself in the kitchen, helping set the food out while he made instant coffee and poured pineapple juice for her daughter.

Instead of handing the gift over and leaving, she ended up staying to share it. Her purpose was not only undermined, but utterly thwarted.

With Suzie in mind, they sat at the pine dining table where any spills could be easily cleaned up. When she had finished her snack, Aaron lifted the child from her chair and gave her a hug.

"I have a box of toys my nephews and niece like to play with," he said. "Would you like to see them?"

He settled her with ease and returned to Kate.

"You should have children of your own," she blurted out. Too late to retrieve the words, she searched his face. "I'm sorry. I didn't mean to—"

He smiled and held up a hand. "I'll take it as a compliment. I love kids. God willing, I'd like to be a father one day."

Something in his eyes made her wonder if he was thinking of forming a family with her, of becoming a father to Suzie. Kate quickly changed the subject, uneasy with the direction of her thoughts.

"Part of the reason for the muffins was to thank you for taking me to work all this time," she said. She finally managed to speak the words she had come to say. "From now on, I'll be able to take care of myself."

He shook his head. "It was no trouble at all. In fact, I'll miss your company on those drives."

She dared not admit she would miss his.

❦

That visit left a strong impression on Kate. She couldn't stop remembering the time they had shared, the three of them comfortable and relaxed inside Aaron's home. It would pop into her mind at odd moments, giving her a warm feeling she couldn't shake off.

Kate parked the Volkswagen in the lot outside the warehouse suite and walked inside. Aaron sat at the desk in the small office.

"Not working outside today?" she asked.

Aaron returned her smile. "We're all on separate jobs today. I wanted to get some of this ready for you," he waved a sheaf of papers in the air, "before I load the truck."

The skin around his eyes crinkled, and he rubbed his hands together. "I start a job at one of the new houses in Pinnacle Estate later this morning."

Kate leaned against the doorjamb. "It's a wrought-iron

fence, isn't it?" she asked shrewdly.

He looked startled. "How did you know that? You haven't even seen the paperwork for it yet. I processed the quote myself."

She stepped fully into the room and smiled down into his face where he sat with the chair tipped back slightly. "You love your work, and you always look forward to starting a new job, but I've come to recognize a special gleam that appears only when it's wrought-iron work."

He grinned before he vacated her chair. "You know me too well. Better get on to it, I guess."

She drew in a breath as they shuffled places in the small space. "Don't you want to show me exactly what you'll be doing?"

He shot her a wry glance. "You enjoy teasing me, don't you?" His laughter was aimed at himself. "Okay, I admit I would like to show you the plans."

He drew them out of a pile on the desk and leaned over her shoulder to lay them down.

Kate tried to concentrate on his words, but her mind kept wandering. He smelled of cool air and the outdoors and stood close enough that she could touch him without even trying.

"So that's about it," Aaron concluded.

She looked at him, hoping he couldn't tell she had been distracted. "I know you'll do a great job. Will you drive me past when it's finished? I'd love to see it."

"Absolutely."

He went off to the far end of the suite, whistling. Kate watched him until he disappeared behind a wall of fencing supplies, and then she settled in to work.

While he searched the other end of the warehouse suite for materials for the new fencing job, she worked on the invoices. Business had picked up as winter drew to a close, and there was plenty to keep her occupied.

When a person telephoned with an important message for Aaron, she sought him out amid the stacks of materials, climbing over a pile of planks toward him and glancing about at the piles of supplies.

"Kate, that's unstable!"

Aaron's warning came at the same moment some loose planks slid beneath her feet and above her, where they had apparently been resting on each other. The domino effect of the loosened materials brought a large pile of lumber crashing downward.

The bulk of the lumber was headed straight for her. At least Aaron was safely on the other side of the crashing planks. Trying to regain her footing to flee, she cried silently for God's help.

Just then Aaron threw himself into the path of the falling wood to sweep her to safety.

As they recovered from the encounter, it seemed natural for his arms to fold around her in comfort.

"That was close." His hand shook slightly as he stroked her hair.

Shocked by the sense of security she felt in Aaron's arms, Kate spoke through trembling lips. "What would have happened if you couldn't get far enough away? All that lumber would have crushed you. I've lost too many people—"

His glance was warm, filled with understanding, and touched with hope. "The Lord was watching over us. We're safe."

❦

Kate kissed her daughter good-bye, thanked Marie again, and turned away. It felt strange to leave Suzie for a whole Saturday, but Aaron had insisted she do this. He had been such a good and understanding employer. How could she refuse to give up just one free day to help him out?

She took one final glance at Marie's spring flower borders, opened the single button on her burgundy jacket, and climbed into the truck.

Aaron started the engine. "All set?"

His lightheartedness caused her to smile. "Yes, I'm all set."

His mood was so infectious, she simply gave herself up to enjoying the day. They chose the new furnishings he wanted for the office, left the truck in an all-day parking lot to travel across Sydney Harbour by ferry, and then shopped and visited an Aboriginal arts museum.

They ate a lunch of Dory fillets and chips on a bench seat overlooking the harbour. Seagulls squawked greedily as they watched for tidbits. A man busked on a didgeridoo, entertaining the tourists.

Aaron turned to her. "This is fun!"

"I'm enjoying it too," she said, smiling.

He leaned forward to look into her eyes. "I'm glad."

They sat for a long time, soaking up the atmosphere, watching people stroll or rush about. The sun had dipped low in the sky when he spoke again.

"You never have told me about your life, Kate."

She met his serious gaze reluctantly. "You know a lot of things. The apparel manufacturing course I want to complete, the places Suzie and I have lived, the jobs I've had."

He shook his head. "There's a big chunk of your life missing in all of that."

She guessed the time had come to tell him. At least it would settle matters between them once and for all. That thought should have comforted her but didn't. "I'm not sure I want to tell you about my marriage."

"You must have loved him a great deal," Aaron murmured.

Kate weighed her words carefully before she spoke. She sent up a silent prayer for God's help. "I was young and inexperienced, but I did love him. My grandmother, my only relative, had just died, and I felt lost and scared. He filled a void in my life."

She drew a deep breath and focused on a distant point of the harbour. "For awhile after we married, I thought things were fine. I left my studies at college because David wanted me at home. When I discovered I was expecting Suzie, he seemed happy."

She ran a hand through her hair, reining in old emotions. It was over now, in the past. Talking about it would never be pleasant—that was all.

Aaron lifted her hand into his. "What happened then?"

"David started to behave oddly," she recalled. "When we first met, I believed he was a strong Christian man, but somewhat silent about his faith. It wasn't until later that I realized he'd only acted that part to please me. Once we'd been married awhile, he saw no reason to continue the farce.

"He started to stay out late at night. Sometimes he didn't come home until morning. He took out a loan and bought a big motorcycle," she said with a sigh, remembering. "A Tone Lazer Red, Springer Softail, to be exact. He was so proud of that bike."

Aaron nodded. "And when Suzie arrived?"

She watched a bank of low-lying clouds scud across the harbour. "I tried to talk to David about his activities, about the people he was spending time with. He wouldn't listen, and the friction over it drove a permanent wedge between us."

She drew a deep breath. It was hard to go on, but too late to stop, now that she had told him this much. "One night Suzie had been crying a lot. David said he couldn't stand the noise, that he had to get out. He left the house without my even trying to tell him good-bye. And that night he rode his motorcycle into a concrete pylon. He didn't have a chance."

Aaron's hand squeezed hers. "It wasn't your fault."

She nodded. "I know that now, but going through that, losing him the way I did, has changed me. All the time we were together I prayed and prayed for God to change him, to help him, but all He did was let him die.

"I did love David. That's the problem. I loved him, I let him become important in my life, and then I lost him, just like my grandmother and my parents. I don't want to suffer any more loss."

She looked into his eyes and said the words that had to come. "I couldn't face loving and losing someone again. I just don't think I'm strong enough."

Aaron sighed and released Kate's hand. He longed to tell her that none of this was God's fault, but he knew she had to discover that for herself. "It's okay, Kate. I understand."

At least now he understood why it was important for him to be patient, to give her the time she needed. She was still healing inside. He had to be careful not to get in the way of the work the Lord was doing in her.

Determined to change the mood, to take her mind off the painful memories his question had raised, he stood up quickly and extended his hand to her. "It's time we got going. I have a plan—to introduce you to the best Italian food in town!"

Kate, silent a moment, rallied to meet him. "As long as you don't try to make me eat pizza with anchovies on it, I don't mind."

They used his cell phone to check on Suzie before they reached the restaurant. Kate talked to her daughter, then Marie. After the call she wore a wry expression on her face.

"Suzie is having such a great time that she wants to stay all night," Kate said. "I guess she's not pining away for me."

Aaron caught her hand briefly. "Then we can enjoy ourselves with a good conscience."

They were laughing as they left the quay, but Aaron's heart was heavy. Their relationship would never move past friendship unless Kate believed she could risk loving again. For that to happen she had to regain her faith in God.

Please help Kate see how much You love her, Lord, Aaron silently prayed. He was learning something, too—to trust and wait for God.

He tried to make the rest of Kate's day pleasant. On the return ferry ride, he kept her above decks, where they discussed the history of the Harbor Bridge, the Sydney Opera House, and some of the other buildings he recognized on the shoreline.

When they passed over the headlands, the ferry dipped into the swell. It wasn't too rough, but Kate wasn't accustomed to sea travel.

"Would you rather go in?" he asked.

She shook her head, her hair curling a little from the damp spray. "I'm fine. Look over there, where the sun has turned the clouds pink and red. Isn't it beautiful?"

It was beautiful, but he found himself studying Kate more often than the view.

Aaron took her to Christina's, a small, informal Italian restaurant. He raised the menu and smiled. "For a taste sensation you'll remember, I recommend the Pasta Ammuddicata."

Kate glanced at the menu, read the description of the meal, and lifted accusing eyes to him. "Pasta Ammuddicata is noodles with anchovy sauce and crisp fried crumbs! I think I'll pass."

She pretended to swat him with her table napkin, and he captured her hand in his.

"I'm sorry. I couldn't resist." He raised an eyebrow. "You know, anchovies really aren't that bad once you get used to them."

"I'll take your word for it, thanks."

She chose the Fettucinni Carbonara—flat noodles served with a creamy bacon sauce. He ordered the same for himself. The waitress returned minutes later with hot foccacia bread.

After Aaron gave thanks for the food, Kate broke off a piece of the bread.

"How did you find this place?"

"Grandma brought me here a couple of years ago. You know how she loves all kinds of foods."

Kate's eyes misted. "She reminds me a lot of my own grandmother."

"Tell me about her," Aaron said, leaning forward.

Kate's voice softened as she spoke of the woman who had raised her from babyhood. "She always managed to make things fun. No matter how hard up we were or how much pressure was on her, she kept smiling and loving."

"She sounds special," Aaron said.

Kate nodded. "Yes. Not everyone would take on sole responsibility of a two-year-old and throw themselves into it the way she did."

"What happened to your parents?" he asked.

"They went to Papua, New Guinea, on a short-term missions trip with some other members of their church. Because of my age, I stayed behind with my grandmother. Dad worked in construction and Mum as a nurse, so their expertise was needed. On a boat trip up the coast near Madang, they were swept out to sea by a storm."

She sighed and blinked. "Everyone on the boat died."

Aaron laid a hand over hers. "I'm so sorry."

When she looked back up at him, she wore a smile. "My grandmother gave me everything a child could hope for. I don't think anyone could give more constant love and support than she did."

❦

Kate should have been happy. She had a good job, a great home to live in, financial security for herself and her daughter. Yesterday's trip to Sydney had ensured a good relationship with Aaron—one of friendship only, which was exactly what she had told herself she wanted.

She reminded herself of the reasons to be thankful as she faced her pale reflection in the bathroom mirror and later as she drove to Marie's to pick up Suzie.

Marie took one glance at her. "You look awful. What happened?"

Kate looked into Marie's warm brown eyes and saw Aaron. Just as she had across the breakfast table this morning when she tried to make small talk with Grandma Bennet. Everywhere she turned, he filled her thoughts. As if that wasn't bad enough, she had to face him in church in about an hour.

"I'm fine, Marie, just tired. Where's Suzie? I hope she was good for you last night."

Marie led the way through the house to the family room, where Suzie was playing a game with the three Baxter children. "Mummy's here, Suzie."

Suzie glanced up. "Hi, Mama."

Marie laughed and gestured toward the kitchen. "Let's have some coffee. We have time, and I don't think you'll budge her until she's finished."

Kate followed reluctantly and hoped Marie would refrain from probing. She simply wasn't up to it today—or so she thought. Somehow she ended up telling Marie the reason for her unhappiness.

"I've come to care deeply about Aaron," Kate admitted. "Until this morning I'd been fooling myself about my feelings, but I can't pretend any longer. I didn't want this."

Marie twirled her empty cup for a moment before she looked up again. "If you care for him, Kate, and he cares for you, then I don't understand what the problem is."

Kate shook her head. "First of all, I don't know if he feels that way toward me. I can't be certain—"

"Have you told him how you feel?" Marie asked.

Kate lowered her gaze. "Marie, I don't want—"

Marie's voice came, gently insistent as she interrupted. "Have you told Aaron how you feel?" she repeated.

"No," Kate said firmly. "He mustn't ever know." She gripped Marie's arm across the table. "Promise me you won't tell him."

Marie shook her head and frowned. "It's not my place to tell him, Kate, and I won't. You owe it to both Aaron and yourself to be honest about this, to give the relationship a chance."

"I can't let myself," Kate said, tears forming in her eyes. "Every adult I've loved, I've lost. I can't face that again."

Marie shook her head again. "I think you may already love him, Kate. It's probably too late to protect yourself from that, and as for his safety—that's in God's hands, as all our lives are."

"I can't commit myself to him," Kate said, looking down. "I have to stop these feelings."

Marie gave a humorless laugh. "How do you propose to do that? Once you give your heart to someone, it's not an easy thing to take it back."

"Oh, Marie, I'm sorry. I didn't mean to bring up painful thoughts for you."

Marie waved her words aside. "For all I know, my problems could be simply in my mind, the product of an overactive imagination and an absent husband. Right now we're talking about you, though, not me."

Kate exhaled her breath on a shaky sigh. "I don't know how I can stop caring for him, but I have to."

Marie laid a hand on her arm. "Have you talked with the Lord about this?"

"Constantly," Kate said, looking up at Marie. "My prayers

seem to go around in circles and not get anywhere. Sometimes I wonder if He's listening, and then I feel bad for thinking that way when I know better."

Marie squeezed her arm and released her. "He always listens. I'll pray about your situation, too. The Lord will show you the way."

seven

Aaron smoothed the partially carved piece of wood beneath his fingertips. When he worked on the portrait-sized photo frame, it helped him stay focused.

After their day in Sydney, he had come home almost convinced there was no hope for him and Kate. Too disheartened to do much more than mutter a few disjointed sentences in prayer, he had yielded the situation to the Lord and gone to bed.

No lightning flash of insight came, but for some reason he began to feel more hopeful about the future. He thought back over their relationship and saw how, despite the obstacles, including not always doing what he knew was right, the Lord had taught him a patience that would hold him in good stead in many of life's future situations.

"Kate is afraid she'll get hurt again," he muttered as he set to carving a star-shaped wildflower on the oval frame. "I have to help her find the faith to embrace our relationship, rather than run from it."

He wanted to see this frame hanging over his mantle, with a picture of the three of them inside—Kate, Suzie, and him.

When he had finished the star, he packed the frame away and drove to work.

❦

It wasn't like Kate to be late. Aaron had his hand on the

phone to call his grandmother when he heard the familiar sound of Kate's car turning into the yard. He met her at the door, and his gaze skimmed Suzie before it returned to Kate in silent question.

"Aaron, Aaron!"

As Kate began her explanation, he scooped the child into his arms. He loved Suzie as if she were his own.

"Grandma was called out early this morning to the Stewarts'." Kate drew a couple of steadying breaths. "Their aunt Claire passed away during the night. Grandma has only just managed to get away. She was upset. I didn't like to leave until I'd seen her safely on her way."

Aaron glanced at Suzie and pointed into the office. "That's where your mama works. Why don't you wait inside? We'll join you in a minute."

Once Suzie was inside where she couldn't hear them, he turned to Kate. "Is Grandma okay?"

Kate nodded, still looking unsettled. "She plans to spend the day with the family. I'm sorry to bring Suzie to work, but I knew Marie wasn't available to care for her today, and I didn't have time to look for anyone else. Besides, I don't like the idea of leaving her with strangers."

Aaron pushed his hands into his pockets. "If we weren't so busy, I'd suggest you take the day off, but there are several jobs I really hoped to get quotes out on today."

She nodded. "That's what I thought too. I'm sure she'll be fine. I've brought things for her to do."

"I have to check on something at one of the sites," Aaron said. "Why don't I take her with me? It'll be only about an hour. That way you can get a good start without any distractions."

"Would you, Aaron?" she asked thankfully. "That would be really helpful, if you're sure it won't be too much trouble."

Trouble? He smiled. "No trouble at all."

She returned the smile and stepped into the office to speak to Suzie. "Would you like to go with Aaron to look at one of his fences, Honey?"

Suzie sprang up from her seat on the floor. "Yes, please!"

Aaron zipped Suzie's thick outdoor coat, waited while she kissed her mama good-bye, and then bundled her into the truck.

"Wouldn't you like to go on your motorbike?" Suzie asked innocently. She was very clever for her age.

Aaron laughed and shook his head. "Not this time, Honey."

He didn't tell her he planned to sell it. Since Kate had shared the story of her past, all desire to ride it had left him. She may have put the memories behind her, but he had no intention of accidentally resurrecting them. The bike didn't mean that much to him.

The site sat on the northern edge of town. Aaron's men had experienced some problems with the client in the early stages of the job. Those matters had been resolved, but Aaron followed any difficult job through closely to ensure that his customers were satisfied and his employees were treated fairly on the work site.

He stopped the truck outside the cabin-style home. "Here we are."

Suzie's eyes widened when she saw the array of small-scale windmills that graced the yard. "Pinwheels!"

Aaron laughed and took Suzie's hand. "They're windmills. On farms they're used to pump water from place to place. Sometimes they're used to catch the wind and make electricity. These are just for show. See how fast they spin around?"

When Aaron had satisfied himself that both his men and the client were happy with the progress, he scooped Suzie into his arms to leave.

"Let's see the windmills again," Suzie said.

She squirmed in his arms, but he held firm as he passed the colorful whirling mills.

"Your mama will be expecting us," he explained. "I'd like to get a treat on the way back and still be on time."

The thought of a treat distracted Suzie from the windmills and allowed him to get her out of the biting wind that had already turned her cheeks cherry red.

The minute they stepped into the warehouse suite, Suzie ran to Kate's desk and plopped the brown paper bag down. "Guess what we bought, Mama!"

Kate sniffed the air and pretended puzzlement. "My guess is—it's a bag of broccoli."

Suzie giggled. "No, Mama!"

Kate raised her eyebrows. "No? Is it spinach then? Squash? Bell peppers? Asparagus?"

"No, Mama!" Suzie clapped her hands. "It's donuts."

They shared the pastries, and then Aaron reluctantly rose to his feet. He would have preferred to spend all day with the two girls, but duty called.

"I probably won't be back until after you've left, Kate," he said. "Call me on the cell phone if you need me for anything."

Kate returned to her work, and Suzie soon became restless. After listening to her insistent hints, Kate took her next door to meet the owners of the motorcycle shop and the camping goods store, who had become her friends in recent weeks.

Afterward she told her daughter firmly that Mama needed to concentrate on her work. "Show me what a lovely picture you can make with your colored pencils."

Outside the wind gradually picked up until it whistled through the rafters of the warehouse. Kate's fingers clicked across the keys as she hurried to complete the last quote. One of the work vehicles came and left again.

As she hit the print key on the computer, Kate smiled and spoke to her daughter without looking up. "I'm all finished. I just need to pack up, and we can leave. I'm sure Aaron won't mind if I close up early."

When Suzie didn't answer, Kate turned in her chair. How much time had passed since she'd last checked on her? Two minutes, ten? Her breath caught in her throat as she stared at the empty space where Suzie had played. The pencils and her coat lay forgotten on the floor.

"She's probably looking at the materials at the other end of the suite," Kate told herself. "I'll just check."

A few minutes later, Kate had searched the whole suite thoroughly. Dread clutched at her throat. "She must have slipped out to one of the other shops."

A blast of cold wind hit Kate as she stepped outside. The sky had turned an angry black. Thunder rumbled overhead.

She hurried into the suite next door. "Did Suzie come in here? Have you seen her?"

They hadn't seen her since Kate brought her in earlier. Nobody else had seen her either.

Dear Lord, where is my baby?

In her fear for Suzie's safety, Kate forgot any thought that the Lord might not be listening. If she had felt distant from Him in the past, it was because of her own fears and uncertainties. Deep in her heart she knew He always listened, always cared.

She rushed back into the office. Her fingers shook as she pressed the numbers to phone Aaron.

"Suzie is missing." She drew a sharp breath. "I've searched everywhere. I don't know where she could be, and there's a storm—"

She heard a sharp intake of breath before he spoke.

"Don't panic," he said. "We'll find her. Have you phoned the police yet?"

"No."

"Do that while you wait for me," he said. "I'll be with you in five minutes."

Kate punched in the number with shaking fingers. She quickly relayed the problem. The police officer assured her that all available officers would be dispatched to begin the search immediately.

As she waited, two of the men from the motorcycle shop came inside. "Have you found your little girl?"

"No," she said raggedly, moved by the kind concern on the weathered faces. "I can't think where she could be."

"We'll close the shop and help you search," the older man said. "You phoned the police?"

As the men left, Aaron and several police officers arrived. Tears filled her eyes as Aaron rushed to her side. His hand on her arm gave comfort.

"Kate Long?"

She turned to the uniformed officer. "Yes. It's my daughter

who has disappeared. I should have watched her more closely. I—"

Aaron squeezed her arm. "This is not your fault, Kate. Let's give the officer the details he needs for the search."

She let out a shuddery sigh. "Of course."

She told the officer the events that had preceded Suzie's disappearance while the man studied a recent photo pulled from her purse. Each moment that passed increased Kate's tension. While they talked, anything could be happening to Suzie.

"Dear Lord!" The cry broke from Kate's lips.

Aaron's arm came around her. "She'll be okay. You mustn't let yourself—"

"You're right." Kate straightened up. "I'm sorry. It's just that Suzie knows she mustn't leave my sight. She's sometimes willful, but I've told her over and over since the day she ran away from me at the mall. I can't understand why she would disappear this way."

The police were anxious to find Suzie before the impending storm hit. In minutes the search operation got under way.

Kate and Aaron left in his truck to search all the places they thought might interest Suzie, while the police, Aaron's workers, and the men from next door began to scour the area.

Aaron laid a hand over both of hers where they lay clenched in her lap. "There's someone on duty at the suite just in case," he said. "He'll contact us immediately if she turns up."

Kate nodded. A dreadful ache settled in her chest. "We've got to find her," she whispered.

"We will," Aaron promised.

As they searched for the next hour, Kate could only pray, "Please, God," over and over. They checked all the shops at the mall, the small park near Grandma Bennet's, the house and grounds themselves in case Suzie had decided to go home for some reason. Desperation threatened to overwhelm Kate when they searched the last place she could think of and failed to find her daughter.

The first heavy gusts of rain against the windshield of the truck brought a fresh wave of concern. "I don't like it that Suzie is out in this bitter weather. Too much time has passed already." Fingers of anxiety clutched at her heart. "She doesn't even have her coat on."

"Wherever she is, the Lord is watching over her," Aaron said quietly.

His words brought some measure of comfort.

"Yes." Kate closed her eyes as she tried to think of other places Suzie might have gone. "Let's search around Marie's house. It's such a long way away, but we should look anyway."

The driving rain made it impossible to see past the sides of the road. Kate's spirits sank further at the hopelessness of the situation. When a search of Marie's place failed to find Suzie, they returned to the warehouse suite.

They learned that the search had fanned wider and had now almost reached the extremities of the town.

The anguish Kate felt stared back at her from Aaron's eyes as they looked at one another.

"If she gets out into the bush, we might never find her," Kate whispered.

"We will find her," Aaron insisted.

Images of her daughter roaming alone amidst the dense foliage of trees, shrubs, and ferns made Kate groan. What if she slipped down a ravine? She could be lying unconscious somewhere right now. How would they find her?

Please, Lord.

They returned to the truck and drove slowly through the sodden streets, stopping at intervals to climb out and call Suzie's name. Rain funneled inside Kate's weatherproof slicker and soaked her neck and sweater, but she didn't care. She had to find her daughter.

When that search also proved fruitless, she climbed back into the vehicle beside Aaron and covered her face with her hands.

"I've lost my baby," she sobbed. "I've lost her."

Aaron's voice broke with emotion as he tried to comfort her. "Hush, my dear. We'll find her."

Kate shook her head. "It's all my fault. I didn't pay attention to her. I just ignored her while I rushed to get through the work so we could go home. If I had checked more often, this wouldn't have happened."

Aaron touched her arm. "It's not your fault, Kate. Don't blame yourself." He drew a deep breath. "Grandma will be home by now. She left her friends when I called her, and she'll be praying, as we both are. Why don't I take you home while I continue to search?"

Kate gave a deep shudder. "I need to be with you. Please, I can't bear it—"

Aaron touched a finger to her cheek. "I won't make you stop searching. I just don't want this to become unbearable for you."

Kate sat up straight. "I'll be all right."

The search was called off for a time after midday. The rain now fell in heavy sheets that made driving unsafe and vision beyond the small arc of the driving lights impossible.

They climbed wearily into the truck to make the crawling journey to Mrs. Bennet's.

Kate turned her face to the bleakness outside. "What's happened to my baby?"

Grandma met them at the door. Her face reflected her tension. "Kate, I'm so sorry. If only I'd stayed home today—"

Kate shook her head, unable to speak. Her body felt numb, her mind and heart one big aching void.

Aaron reassured his grandmother. "It's nobody's fault, Grandma. Kate was grateful to know you were praying while we searched, and you had to attend to your friends."

Kate managed a nod before her lips began to tremble. Despite the weariness Aaron must have also felt, his strong arms gathered her close.

"You need to dry off and eat."

She shook her head. "I can't—Suzie—I have to do something—"

When he replied, his voice held a stern edge she wasn't accustomed to hearing. "You'll help her best by keeping your strength up for when she's found."

Kate's gaze drifted upward to his taut features until she found the deep compassion in his eyes.

This had hurt Aaron too. "Yes, of course. I'm sorry."

She allowed Grandma to lead her away. In the privacy of her room, her tears flowed. Her mood was somber when she returned to the kitchen minutes later.

"Do you have any news?" she asked immediately.

Aaron shook his head, and her heart plummeted again.

"No, nothing yet," he said.

He had changed into the dry clothes he kept in the truck for emergencies. Kate looked at him and wished she could tell him in words how much his presence had meant to her today.

"You'll have some soup, won't you, my dear?" Grandma asked.

Kate turned slowly. "I don't think I can eat."

The older lady insisted, and Kate did feel slightly better once she had forced a few mouthfuls of the creamy liquid down her throat.

Grandma's hand came out to cover hers on the table. "Pastor Tony has started a prayer vigil at the church. They won't stop until our baby is found. Have faith in the Lord, Kate. I know it's hard."

Kate tried to keep her faith strong as the time crept by. It was difficult to remain seated on Grandma's sofa when she wanted to be out there, doing something.

Grandma's eyes remained closed as her lips moved in silent prayer.

When Kate allowed her hand to creep into Aaron's, he turned to her.

"The moment the rain eases enough for us to see," he promised, "we'll go out again. Remember what He says—'I will never leave you nor forsake you.' Wherever Suzie is, He is with her."

Grandma Bennet had said the same thing to her some time ago. Kate wanted to believe it.

The phone rang as they were leaving the house twenty minutes later. They stayed long enough to confirm their plans with the police and climbed back into the truck.

"We'll do a systematic search of the places we've already looked," Aaron said. "If she's moving around, we could find her anywhere."

Kate drew a deep breath. "Let's start with the mall then, and we'll check our old apartment building again too."

They both kept their eyes trained on the sides of the road as they drove. Kate's tension built to almost unbearable proportions as she tried not to think of the things that could have happened to her daughter.

"I'll never let her out of my sight again," she said with determination.

Aaron nodded.

Their tour of the mall and the old apartment building proved fruitless. Suzie wasn't there. Nobody remembered seeing a child of her description. Most folks had gone home to keep out of the weather.

When they climbed back into the truck, Aaron slapped his open hand against the steering wheel. "We must be missing something."

He gripped Kate's hands in his and closed his eyes. "Dear Lord Jesus, please help us. We don't know where else to look."

His voice broke on the last words, and Kate whispered a shaky "amen."

They sat for a moment with their foreheads touching, before Aaron eased back to look into her eyes. "Let's go back to the warehouse. I feel like we need to."

They stepped into the small office, disheartened but not surprised when they received no fresh news.

Kate fought the tears back as she leaned over to pick up Suzie's coat and press it to her face.

She looked up as Aaron reached down beside her.

He unfolded a small sheet of paper. "Did Suzie draw this today?"

Kate glanced at the picture and nodded. "It must have been in her coat pocket. She was drawing before she—disappeared."

Aaron pointed at the round blobs and sticks. "I wonder what these are?"

She frowned. "Flowers? No, some of them have pointy bits sticking out. I wonder what—"

Suddenly Aaron clamped his fingers around her arm. "Windmills. Could they be windmills?"

Kate's heart began to thump as she studied the picture more closely. "I guess they could be, but where would she have seen—?"

Aaron pulled her toward the door. "Come on! I think I know where she might be. I'll explain on the way!"

eight

Aaron drove as fast as safety permitted.

"I don't want to waste a moment," he said. "The home we visited this morning has a whole bunch of decorative windmills in the yard. Suzie was fascinated by them. When it was time to leave, she wanted to stay. It was only the thought of a treat that convinced her otherwise. I'm sure that's where she must be."

Kate whispered a prayer as they pulled up in front of the house. "I hope you're right!"

They leapt from the truck, calling Suzie's name. Another downpour soaked them in seconds and just as suddenly disappeared. Kate hardly noticed.

The porch stood empty. No lights shone from the house. While Aaron pounded on the front door, Kate hurried to check the side of the building.

Aaron rejoined her quickly. "There's nobody home."

Kate leaned into the strength of his firm grip as she struggled over the muddy ground. "Maybe around back?"

They checked the rear of the property and continued to call Suzie's name.

Around the second side of the house, they found an empty bird enclosure and a small vegetable garden.

"She has to be here." Kate drew a breath over the raw feeling in her throat. "Let's check the front again."

"Suzie! Where are you, Honey? Please come out to Mama," she cried.

A faint sound of childish weeping. Kate wasn't sure if she had heard it or if she had made it up out of the desperation she felt. She gripped Aaron's arm. "Did you hear that?"

"Suzie?" She drew in another breath. "Suzie!"

Aaron shouted Suzie's name too. They both ran to the rear of the building, where the sound seemed to have come from.

A pile of blue tarp covers stirred, and a small, tear-streaked face appeared.

"Suzie!" Kate rushed to her daughter, clasped the child against her, and held the shivering body tightly. "Thank You, Lord. Thank You!"

She felt the warmth and fierceness of Aaron's clasp, as he wound his arms around her and her daughter. The tremors that coursed through his body echoed her own.

Suzie lifted tear-stained eyes. "I'm sorry, Mama. I was bad, wasn't I? And then the men didn't come back."

Kate frowned down at her daughter.

"What men?" she demanded. "Did they hurt you?"

"No, Mama." Suzie shook her head. "Aaron's work-mens wouldn't hurt me," she declared. She looked at Kate as if to insinuate her mother had lost her good sense.

"She must have hidden in the truck when they came back to the warehouse," Kate murmured.

"And she was left behind when they finished here," Aaron added.

"I was scared. Then I got all wet and cold." She broke into noisy sobs.

Despite her efforts to hold them back, Kate's tears dropped onto her daughter's head as Aaron led them to the truck.

He cleared his throat. "Let's get her inside and let the others know we've found her."

In the moments it took for him to make the call on his cell phone, Kate huddled her daughter close. Holding her was the best thing Kate had done all day.

As Aaron finished the phone call, she looked at him. "What would I have done without you?"

With her words came another wave of emotion that sent fresh tears from her eyes. "Oh, Aaron—"

He stroked a finger down her cheek, then her daughter's, before he buckled them in and eased the truck onto the road. "Do you want her checked by a doctor?"

"No." Kate drew a calming breath. "Let's get her straight home and into a hot bath. Hopefully she won't catch worse than a cold out of this. We can always call a doctor to the house, if there's a need."

"You're soaked again too," Aaron pointed out.

Kate sensed his concern as he surveyed her. Her hair hung in straggly clumps. She could only imagine how bad she must look.

"I'll be fine," she said. "Suzie is the one who needs the attention."

Kate felt numb by the time Aaron parked the truck outside Grandma's house. Kate followed quietly as he carried Suzie inside, where he assured his grandmother that Suzie was chilled but unharmed.

"The Lord be praised!"

Grandma's misty eyes were too much for Kate. She turned aside as she fought for her own control.

"We're all thankful." Aaron quietly passed Suzie into Kate's waiting arms.

Kate left him to comfort the older lady while she tended to her daughter's needs.

The tub of gardenia-scented water appealed to Suzie at

once. She eagerly allowed herself to be plunged into the warming depths. Once in the water, she confessed how much she had wanted to return to look at the windmills.

Kate caught her daughter's soapy hands in hers for a moment. "Do you understand now, Suzie, why Mama tells you not to run off? I must always know where you are so I can do my best to keep you safe."

The child nodded solemnly. "I'm sorry, Mama."

Kate rinsed the remainder of the soap from Suzie's wiggly body and lifted her from the tub. "Good girl. Are you hungry?"

Suzie rubbed her stomach as Kate dressed her in dry clothes. "I could eat everything in the whole world!" she declared.

"Then let's dry your hair, and we'll go find you some food," Kate said. "I think Grandma will have something yummy waiting in the kitchen."

Suzie fell quiet as the hair dryer hummed, and Kate's thoughts turned to Aaron. He had been her rock throughout the long hours of Suzie's disappearance.

Aaron had shared her concern and worry; yet he had never once given up or lost sight of their goal as they searched for her daughter.

While her faith wavered, his had held firm. "I'm sorry I doubted, Lord. Thank You for taking care of Suzie while she was lost. Thank You for Aaron too."

Kate switched the dryer off and gave Suzie's hair a final brush.

Aaron glanced at her wet clothing with concern when she appeared, so Kate left Suzie at the door of the kitchen and turned back to the bathroom.

"You're wet too," she called over her shoulder.

Aaron would have smiled if his heart hadn't felt so full of emotion. He found it hard enough just to breathe. What a time for Kate to assert herself!

He excused himself quickly to his grandmother and left. As he climbed into the truck, he noticed the weather had almost cleared now. The rain had stopped, and the residue of cloud scudded away.

Once inside his house, he closed the front door and leaned heavily against it. The moment he shut his eyes, images of Suzie lost and alone in the storm besieged him.

When he tried to say a prayer of thanks, he could only manage a few stumbling words before emotion threatened his composure again.

A voice within seemed to caution him to stay home and let some time pass before he saw Kate again. He felt raw and exposed and uncertain if he could control the feelings that whirled within.

Yet, caution or no caution, he couldn't stay away.

Showered and dry once more, he stood back outside his grandmother's less than thirty minutes later. When she opened the door, the house remained quiet behind her. For a moment he looked into the old lady's far-seeing eyes.

Then he leaned down to receive her comforting hug. "Oh, Grandma—"

Her hands patted his back for a moment before she drew back and turned toward the kitchen. "Suzie is sound asleep, poor lamb. I'm sure she won't wake until morning. Come, Dear, let me make you some coffee."

Kate sat at the kitchen table, a steaming mug clasped in her hands. She had changed into a wool dress of light peach. Her hair once again looked glossy and fell straight to her shoulders in a fine curtain.

Aaron wanted to tell her how anxious he had been today, how concerned that somehow he would let her down and not find Suzie.

All the things he wanted to say were locked inside a chest that ached with the burden of his love.

He stood quietly, while Kate surveyed him.

"You look better," she said, her voice low. She gave a satisfied nod.

He heard the huskiness in her voice and scanned her face quickly. "I'm all right," he said. "I only needed to dry out. You, on the other hand, look very pale, and your voice sounds scratchy. How do you feel?"

She gave a wry smile. "Apart from the lump of tension yet to leave my throat and the desire to burst into tears, I'm fine."

Grandma interposed then as she handed him his coffee. "Kate has checked on Suzie every five minutes since the dear child fell asleep."

"I'd like to see her too," he admitted.

He detected understanding in Kate's gaze as she nodded. Neither one of them would want to let the child out of their sight for awhile.

"We can check her together now, if you like," Kate said.

They crept to the doorway of Suzie's room.

The scent of violets floating from Kate's hair melded with the sound of Suzie's soft breaths and the rustle of the wind through the trees outside the window.

This picture would be forever etched in Aaron's memory. Kate at his side, gazing at her daughter with such pride and love. Suzie peacefully asleep, her face relaxed, one small hand pressed under her chin, the other wrapped around a worn yellow stuffed bear.

The scene had a sense of family about it that was the very thing Aaron wanted to embrace for the rest of his life, and only with Kate.

He turned. "Kate—"

She held up a finger. "Wait a moment."

He stood motionless as she crept into the room. His heart stood motionless, too, as she bent to brush a kiss across her daughter's brow.

A powerful surge of love for this woman and her child rushed through him. Hard on its heels came the caution he had worked so hard to find in past days and weeks. Now wasn't the right time to declare his feelings to Kate. It had been an emotional day. She probably felt just as wrung out and vulnerable as he did. He would be taking unfair advantage to bring up personal matters right now.

"What did you want to say?" Kate asked as they returned to the kitchen.

He shook his head. "It can wait. Would you like fresh coffee?"

She nodded absently as she glanced around the kitchen and realized Grandma had left them. "I'll fix it."

Aaron shook his head and indicated the chair she had vacated earlier. "Let me."

He could feel her eyes on him as he rinsed and refilled her mug.

"I can't thank you enough for your support today," she said as he sat down opposite her at the table. "I've spoken to Suzie about going off without me, and I think the episode frightened her enough that she'll remember to obey me in the future. I'll make up the work hours I've lost, of course."

Aaron laid a hand over hers where she had begun to pluck

at the tablecloth. "Don't give the lost hours a thought," he said. "I'm just relieved and thankful that we found Suzie and she's unharmed.

"Actually," he added, "I don't want to see you back at the office until you're certain Suzie has had no unwelcome after-effects from today's soaking. If you need time off for yourself, I want you to take it. The work can wait until you're ready. What you experienced today was very traumatic."

"Thank you, Aaron, so much," Kate murmured.

He might have stayed on his side of the table, if she hadn't reached a trembling hand toward him in mute appeal.

"Kate." He stood up and stepped quickly around the table. "I really need to hold you right now, if I may?"

She felt so fragile as he held her gently in his arms. How could those small shoulders bear so much?

Suddenly he had to articulate what today had done to him. "I don't think I could have borne it if we hadn't found her," he said hoarsely, "or if something bad had happened to her. Every time I shut my eyes, even now, I see all the horrible possibilities."

He dropped his head until his face rested in her hair. They remained like that for a moment before she stepped back.

"I'm glad you—care—about Suzie," she said haltingly. "It means a great deal to me to know that."

Mrs. Bennet entered the kitchen just then. "Time to start dinner," she said, glancing from one to the other.

"Will you stay?" she asked, turning to Aaron.

Kate put her hand on the table to steady herself, looking at Mrs. Bennet and Aaron without seeing either of them.

"I hope you'll excuse me," she said. "I–I think I might lie down for awhile."

She stepped into her bedroom and closed the door, leaning against it for a moment to catch her breath. Then she slumped across her bed.

"Dear Lord, what can I do?"

Had it just been the need to lean on someone that made her feel such closeness with Aaron today? No. It was a lot more than that.

"I lost my confidence and direction and leaned on another person for awhile," she mumbled into the patterned quilt cover. "It didn't have to be Aaron. Anyone would have done."

If that were true, then why had she wanted only his presence during the search for Suzie? Why hadn't she gone with one of the police vehicles?

"You wanted to be with him," she told herself. "Not someone else. Why don't you admit it, face it, instead of trying to push it aside? You love the man, and no matter how hard you try to ignore the fact, it is not going away."

Her head began to ache. She had endured too much tension today already. This inner conflict just made it worse. She gave the pillow a frustrated punch and rolled onto her back.

There were cracks in the ceiling. Little hairline fractures that separated the paint into jagged lines. It reminded her of her life. It looked okay until you got up close, but a detailed inspection revealed the flaws.

Kate could hear the front door open and a few murmured words between Grandma and Aaron. Then the door closed again, and the house fell silent.

Kate slipped off her shoes and climbed under the covers. She had probably imagined the look in Aaron's eyes today anyhow.

❦

Suzie had a temperature the afternoon following her disappearance. By the end of the day, she had succumbed to a head cold. Kate nursed her through it, barely aware of the changes taking place in her own health until one day Suzie had recovered and the time came for Kate to go back to work.

A wave of dizziness washed over her as she arrived at the warehouse suite. She had to grip the side of the car as she climbed out.

The morning passed in a hazy fog. Aaron asked if she felt all right, but she waved him away.

"I'm fine," she insisted. "You go about your business. I have to tackle this backlog."

The pile of invoices slowly decreased. Her feeling of detachment increased. When Aaron returned a little after midday, she tipped her head on one side and frowned.

"There are two of you," she enunciated carefully around her woolly tongue. Then her head fell gently downward.

She woke to find herself tucked in bed. Her body felt as though someone had used it for a trampoline. Her head ached. The interior of her mouth mirrored the parched heat of the Central Australian desert, and her stomach clenched and rumbled ominously.

Kate groaned.

A cool hand brushed her brow, and a straw was placed between her lips. "Take a little water, Kate. That's a good girl."

She identified Grandma's voice and sipped the water, but the drink made her stomach feel worse.

"Just relax, Child," Grandma said. "You've been out of it for two days, but you're starting to mend now."

Grandma's voice soothed her. The rumbling stomach settled, and she started to drift back into sleep, but she had to know something, something important.

"Suzie?"

The word was barely distinguishable, but Grandma understood.

"She's fine, Dear. We're looking after her. Go to sleep now, and when you wake again, you'll feel much better."

"We're looking after her"?

Kate couldn't think.

Sleep claimed her.

The next time she woke, she felt shaky but better. While she ate the spring vegetable soup Grandma brought, she agreed that a bath sounded like what she needed. "What time is it? Did I sleep long? Where's Suzie?"

Tired lines fanned out from Grandma's eyes as she smiled gently. "What a lot of questions. You fell ill on Monday. It's now Thursday afternoon. Suzie is at Marie's house. She hasn't spent the whole time there, but Marie didn't have to work today, so she offered to take her. Other times Aaron has looked after her. We tried to keep her away, as we thought you'd rather she see you when you were fully sensible."

Kate nodded and regretted the sharp movement as needles jabbed inside her head. "Yes, of course. Thank you."

It was hard to believe she had slept so long, completely oblivious to what went on around her.

She did have a recollection, but maybe it was a dream. Had Aaron really stood in the doorway of her room with Grandma? Had she heard him express concern before Grandma ushered him away?

No. He wouldn't have been there, worrying over her. She gave up the struggle to separate the truths and unrealities of the past days. Maybe later it would all make sense.

Kate managed to sit down to dinner with Grandma and Suzie. Afterward she rested in the lounger in the living room and gave Suzie her attention. Her daughter didn't seem upset from the separation, which showed she had been well cared for.

Kate glanced across at where Grandma sat mending a tear in a pink floral blouse. "I do thank you, Grandma, for taking care of me and Suzie. It would have been a disaster without your help."

Grandma shook her head. "It was no trouble, Child. I'm just glad you feel better. The doctor told me that once you got out of bed, you would recover rapidly. It seems he was right."

The doorbell rang.

"Visitors, visitors! Can I get it?" Suzie barely waited for Grandma's permission before she bolted for the front door and swung it open.

Kate had no time to disappear into her room. She gathered the folds of her old sweater closer and hoped it wasn't Pastor Tony or one of the Garden Society ladies.

"Hi, Grandma. I thought I'd come and check in on the invalid."

Oh, his voice sounded so sweet. Kate had missed its sound. Her face warmed as Aaron entered the living room. She wanted to soak in the sight of him.

He looked wonderful.

"Hi, Kate." He smiled and perched on the arm of the

sofa facing her. "It's good to see you looking better."

She forced herself not to pluck at her sweater. How could she have ever thought this strong man could be for her? Weak, unbelieving Kate, who couldn't even trust that God would find her daughter and then collapsed when she should have been protecting her from any further danger.

"Grandma tells me you helped care for Suzie," she said presently. "Thank you for that, and I hope my absence hasn't messed up things at work."

He shook his head. "Not at all." Then he grinned. "Well, a little. I have to admit the customers like to deal with you. The computer doesn't seem to respect me the same way it does you either."

Aaron's humor brought a laugh out of her. Then suddenly he grew quiet, and his eyes took on a serious look.

Kate's laughter faded, too, and her heart fluttered as she absorbed his expression. "What is it?"

He stood to his feet. His fingers combed through his hair in a distracted fashion. "Nothing. I have to be going. I just stopped in to check up on you."

He backed toward the front door and paused, lifting a hand, then dropping it to his side.

She thought she heard him mumble something about not waiting any longer, but she couldn't be sure.

nine

Kate stared at the parchment roll that sat beside her breakfast place setting. While Grandma busied herself at the sink, Kate pulled off the piece of red ribbon and unfurled it. Inside was Grandma's recipe for chicken and seafood casserole.

Kate's heart fluttered as she recognized Aaron's handwriting and realized he must have left the parchment.

She looked at Grandma. "Did you ask Aaron to write this for me?" she asked, with a catch in her voice.

"Gracious, no. Aaron slipped in first thing this morning and left it. What is it, Dear? An invitation to something?"

Kate laughed. To her ears the sound came out strained. Didn't the man know she was too weak to resist him if he started paying her special attention? She was having enough trouble working near him. "No. Actually it's a recipe."

She almost smiled as Grandma's eyebrows rose.

"A recipe!" Grandma exclaimed. "For what?"

"For your chicken and seafood casserole."

Grandma reached for her reading glasses where they rested on top of her head and indicated the scroll. "May I, Dear?"

Kate handed it to her. "It just has the recipe and his initials at the bottom. I wonder why he would give me something like that? I could get the recipe directly from you, if I wanted it."

Suddenly Grandma's face cleared, and she handed the parchment back.

"How like Aaron." She broke into a smile. "The first time he met you, I had sent him to the mall for the ingredients of that casserole. I think he might be trying to tell you something, Dear."

Kate didn't know what to say.

"It was just a nice gesture," she declared, as much as a warning to herself as to convince Grandma Bennet. "He knows I like cooking. I expect he thought I'd like to add it to my collection of recipes." She gestured into the air with a feeble wave. "Or something."

Grandma smiled. "Yes, or something."

Kate took the paper into her room after breakfast and pored over the neat script. If Aaron was trying to tell her something, she had to stop it right now. Yet for all her mental protests, she couldn't help feeling a little thrilled that he had done this for her.

I need the strength to resist, Lord.

She fingered the parchment one last time, before she tucked it carefully into the dresser drawer beside her small collection of jewelry.

On Saturday when she slipped outside to retrieve Grandma's newspaper, Kate found a package on the porch beside it. She glanced up and down the street. She saw no sign of Aaron, but she knew it had come from him.

Her heart thumped wildly for a moment. She immediately told herself she should have returned the parchment at once. If she had, she could have prevented the embarrassment of a second gift.

Tucking the newspaper under one arm, she lifted the

small package slowly and stepped back inside. The others were still asleep, so she laid the newspaper on the coffee table and carried the package to her bedroom, shutting the door quietly behind her.

Her fingers trembled a little as she removed the plain brown paper. Inside she found a small figurine that still bore the tag of a local variety store.

It was mass-produced but beautiful. Its smooth lines captured the love of the woman for the child she held in her arms. Holding the ornament to the light, Kate could see the woman's hair almost glowing.

She stared at it for a long time.

As she glanced back down at the box, she noticed a folded sheet of blue paper tucked inside. When she drew it out, she realized it was a church newsletter. Not just any one, but the one from the first service she had attended at Saint Luke's.

She had sat with Suzie in her lap, and Aaron had glanced across the church at her. Later he drove her home in his truck and told her he wanted to see her again.

Had he really seen her as a figure of maternal love, bathed in light?

"It's going straight back," she told herself. "He shouldn't do this kind of thing. If I keep it, I will only encourage him."

She laid the figurine beside the recipe scroll where little fingers couldn't find it and damage it.

By Monday Kate had received two more gifts. An award ribbon from the church talent night and a sprig of holly joined her collection. She had tried to contact Aaron by phone, twice, to ask him to stop sending the gifts, but she hadn't been able to track him down. At church he had slipped away before she could find the courage to go to him and broach the subject.

The gifts made Kate feel very special, and she recognized the danger of that.

"I'll take them with me to work and hand them back," she told herself.

❦

Kate had been watching the door ever since she had arrived at work. Now Aaron was finally here, and her nerves were on edge. His other gifts were tucked away in the desk drawer. It was going to be even harder to give them back than she had thought. He had brought another gift this morning—apple and cinnamon muffins. The spicy smell drifted from the covered platter and filled the small office space.

She saved her file, sat up in her chair, and looked at him.

He looked back at her, a tiny hint of challenge in his expression. "Hi," he said. "I hope you're hungry. They're fresh out of the oven."

"That's nice." She paused as she sought the right words. "Aaron, about all these gifts—"

His eyes were so bright and clear that she felt she could see inside him. A slight smile played at one corner of his mouth as he waited for her to go on.

"You've made me feel very special," she said quietly. "Thank you."

The words rolled off her tongue, husky and unchecked, not at all what she had intended to say.

Kate stopped, appalled.

A pleased smile spread across Aaron's face, making her feel even worse. Why, oh, why hadn't she told him to stop giving her things before this?

A few moments alone to compose her thoughts seemed like a good idea. The microwave oven and sink were housed outside the office in the larger part of the building.

"I'll make the coffee," she muttered hurriedly and escaped past him to put the pot on.

"I'll help," he said, setting the muffins on the desk and turning to follow her.

Even the sound of his footfalls behind her tugged at her heart. She found it hard to concentrate.

No other person was quite like Aaron. He was God's unique creation, different, yet familiar and—dear. Even with her back turned, Kate could imagine his movements as if he were walking in front of her where she could see him.

Aaron paused behind her, waiting until she moved to the left before he reached over her shoulder to take down two coffee mugs. Kate closed her eyes and drew a slow breath.

Aaron's clothing smelled of fresh air and something lemony. The coffee lid rattled as she tried to open it. "I seem to be all thumbs," she mumbled. "I'll just—"

Aaron reached out to help. With one movement he took care of the coffee jar. "Better?"

She nodded. "Thank you."

Aaron tilted his head, watching her thoughtfully.

"I'm so glad your faith has grown so much that you don't feel threatened by my gifts," he said suddenly. "It gives me hope for our future."

Kate wanted to believe God had led her to Aaron because He wanted them to be together. But she didn't know how to tell Aaron of her fears without losing face in front of him. It was probably her pride, but she didn't want him to know how weak her faith really was.

Maybe, if she went along with things for awhile. . .

She took one small step toward him. "I—"

Aaron slowly closed his strong arms around her. With a muttered endearment, he kissed her.

A moment later, trembling inside, Kate stepped back. "I should fix the coffee."

"I'll spread some margarine on the muffins," Aaron offered.

The muffins tasted wonderful, or maybe it was the company that made everything seem special. Kate brushed her doubts aside along with the crumbs on her fingers and smiled as Aaron reached for another muffin.

He grinned sheepishly. "I hope that you haven't been counting."

"Certainly not." She tilted her head to one side. "I had no idea you were such a great cook. Actually, I thought you might not be able to boil water."

He laughed. "I've been cooking since childhood. What made you think I was no good at it? Did Marie tell you I almost burned the kitchen down once when we were kids?"

Kate shook her head, enchanted with the idea of learning about his childhood. "She didn't, but now that you've mentioned it, I'll be sure to ask her for the full story." She paused for a second and met his gaze. "It's just that you were always at Grandma's. I thought you must have needed the home-cooked meals."

His eyes glowed with warmth as he leaned forward in his chair. "What I needed was to be near you. I've been praying for a way to be close to you for a long time, Kate."

Again she wrestled her guilt and fears.

I will not hurt him, she promised herself.

Out loud she said, "I appreciate your telling me that."

Aaron stayed at the warehouse all morning. At the end of Kate's shift, he locked up and followed her to Grandma's. They sat side by side at the kitchen table and ate canned tomato soup and crusty bread rolls.

It was a pleasant time, yet Kate would have been happier if she could shake the doubts that refused to be dislodged.

When they had finished lunch, Aaron squeezed her hand quickly beneath the table.

"How about dinner at my place tonight—you, Grandma, Suzie, and me?" He glanced at his grandmother. "That won't put you out too much, will it?"

Grandma nodded. "Not at all. It would be a pleasure."

Kate couldn't very well say no when his grandmother had already accepted the invitation. "That would be very nice. Thank you."

"Great." Aaron stood. "I'll collect you all when I finish work. I'll try to finish up early and be here by five."

She walked him to the door and then to his truck. Once they were alone, he lifted her and swung her in a circle before setting her down.

"You're beautiful, you know," he murmured, smiling into her eyes.

She shook her head. "No, I—"

He shook a finger and gave her an admonishing glance. "It's only the truth."

When Aaron left, she walked slowly back to the house. She felt trapped and very, very uncertain. Kate snapped her fingers. She would have a little shopping trip and buy herself something to wear. She hadn't had anything new for ages. That was bound to lift her out of the doldrums!

Ferntree Heights had only one clothing store, so Kate piled Suzie into the small car and drove to Lithgow. Grandma Bennet declined her invitation.

"Look, Mama," Suzie said as they browsed in one of the dress shops.

Kate blinked in surprise at the rose pink blouse Suzie held aloft. She had been looking for almost an hour. So far nothing had seemed right, but the blouse was lovely. The sleeves were gathered at the shoulder and tapered from elbow to wrist. A placket hid the row of buttons down the front. Tiny pearl snaps graced collar and cuffs. It even looked like the right size.

"I think I'll try that on," Kate said.

Suzie's eyes widened as a grin spread across her face. "Really?" She danced up and down. "I choosed it! I choosed it!"

"Chose it, Honey," Kate mumbled absently as she headed for a dressing room, towing Suzie behind her.

The blouse fit perfectly.

Kate paid for the purchase and left the shop with a smile. Not so long ago she had been counting every cent and worrying over her future, and now she could afford a new blouse without feeling guilty.

Her life was turning around. She had coped so far, so maybe she could cope with getting closer to Aaron too.

They were all ready when Aaron arrived. True to his word, he had finished work early. Kate opened the door to see him in beige trousers and a brown shirt that deepened the color of his eyes. He smelled of shampoo and chamomile soap.

"Hi," she said.

"You look lovely." Aaron turned to smile at his grandmother as she and Suzie emerged from the living room. "Is everyone ready to leave?"

Kate nodded. "I think we all are."

Aaron helped his grandmother into the front seat of the truck and then Suzie into the back beside Kate.

"I'm looking forward to having you and Suzie visit in my home again," he whispered to Kate.

A wave of pleasure washed over her. "I'm looking forward to it too." She hesitated. "We could have driven ourselves, but you had said you'd pick us up."

Aaron shook his head. "It's my pleasure to do the driving. Besides," he added, closing the door, "this way I get all your company on the drive back as well."

Aaron hadn't exaggerated his culinary skills. While Grandma entertained Suzie, he enlisted Kate's help in making stir-fry chicken with bamboo shoots, baby corn, and snow peas, accompanied by perfect fluffy rice.

During the meal they talked about his business, summer weather in the mountains, and his possible need for another employee to help through the busy season.

"I could always don overalls and come out to help you," Kate offered in a teasing voice, without thinking.

Aaron shook his head. He glanced at his grandmother and back to Kate. "I would be so distracted that I'd end up cementing myself into a post hole or putting a fence up at the wrong house."

A warm flush spread across Kate's face at his open admiration in front of his grandmother.

Later they sat in the living room, talking. Grandma held

Suzie on her lap until the child fell asleep.

"I'll put her down in the spare room," she whispered. As Suzie stirred, she patted the small back gently and rose to her feet.

"Let me carry her," Kate said quickly. "She's too heavy for you."

"Nonsense," Grandma Bennet said quietly. "I'll be back in a moment."

Aaron turned to Kate as his grandmother left the room. "I want to see you more often, Kate," he said. "Outside of the work and family environments. We need to spend some time together so we can get to know each other."

Kate looked at his face, but no words came.

He mistook her speechlessness for a different kind of hesitation and gave a wry smile.

"You know I love Suzie," he said, "and Grandma, and I don't want to take you away from either of them." He paused. "It's just that I think we need to be on our own sometimes. Work isn't the best place to do that."

Kate had to agree, but she still had so many doubts. Surely one or two innocent outings wouldn't do any harm. "Perhaps we could hike one of the trails."

"That would be good," Aaron agreed. "In the meantime, I hope you'll let me take you out to dinner tomorrow evening. We'll go somewhere quiet where we can talk."

That was much more immediate. Kate hesitated and then told herself it would be all right as she heard Grandma Bennet's footsteps in the hall. "I'll have to ask either Grandma or Marie to mind Suzie, but I don't think it will be a problem."

The three of them talked quietly for another hour before

Kate noticed Grandma Bennet's drooping eyelids and declared it was time to go home.

Grandma insisted on riding in the back with Suzie on the way home and was soon dozing.

When Aaron was preparing for bed that evening, he was pleased at the change in his relationship with Kate. It wasn't until much later, though, as he rose from his bed to watch the dawn cascade across the sky, that he realized Kate had not actually committed herself to him in so many words.

He shook his head.

They were meant for each other. He knew it in his heart, and he believed Kate knew it too.

It would be all right.

He pushed aside the niggling sense of doubt that wouldn't seem to leave him.

Nothing would go wrong now. They only needed some quality time together so they could build their relationship.

ten

The phone call came that morning. Aaron's parents had decided to cut short their time in New Zealand and come home. Aaron reorganized his work schedule, called Kate at his grandmother's to explain briefly what was happening and that they would have to cancel their dinner plans, and drove to Sydney to meet his parents' flight.

Once they had arrived, Aaron hustled them into the truck and headed for Ferntree Heights. While his father dozed in the backseat, his mother turned to face him.

"You're rather quiet," she remarked. "I hope this hasn't inconvenienced you too much. Your father and I managed to get a cancellation at the last minute, so we came on."

Aaron shook his head. "I'm glad to see you both," he assured his mother. "Too much time has passed since you were home."

Their arrival came at an uncomfortable time for him, but he was glad to see them. He hadn't realized how much he had missed them until he saw them stepping off the airplane.

The crow's feet at the corners of his mother's eyes deepened as she smiled.

"It certainly feels good to be home again," she said. "I'm sorry to spring it on you like this, but I'm afraid we'll have to ask if you'd mind if we stay with you until Joe and Fiona fly back to New Zealand. I hope that will be all right."

Aaron hadn't given accommodations a thought, and now

his heart sank. He didn't want them to stay with him right now. It would interfere with his plans and make it difficult for him to spend as much time with Kate as he would like.

"Have you been in contact with Joe?" he asked.

His mother folded her hands in her lap. "No, Darling. We couldn't think of doing that. We agreed to a specified period for the house swap. Your father and I don't expect them to cut their visit short just because we got homesick."

"Oh." Aaron struggled to find the welcome that should have naturally arisen in his heart. "That's great then." He tried to inject real warmth into his smile. "We'll have a terrific time together."

For a moment he considered suggesting they stay at Grandma's, but he quickly squashed the thought. There wasn't enough room at Marie's either. If they needed to stay somewhere, it would have to be at his place.

His relationship with Kate was so new and fragile that he wanted to do everything he could to protect it. A flare of impatience washed over him, making him wonder if he had learned as much about "waiting" and "trusting" as he had thought.

The temptation to bulldoze his way through the problem was strong, but he did his best to resist it and reminded himself that God was still in control and knew what He was doing.

Once back in Ferntree Heights, Aaron settled his parents into his home and left them to rest while he went straight to the warehouse suite.

Kate looked even more beautiful than the day before. Her skin glowed with good health, and her hair hung in a spun-gold curtain around her shoulders. His gaze rested on her hands as she deftly flipped through files. He stood silently, accepting that he was deeper in love with her than ever. He wondered if he would always feel this sense of wonder when he watched her and decided he probably would.

"Hi."

Kate looked up from the files she was sorting. There were shadows in her eyes, but her face creased into a smile. He read special warmth for him in her gaze, and it made him glad.

She closed the filing cabinet and took a step toward him. "Is everything okay? How was your parents' flight?"

"Everything is all right," he conceded. "Mum and Dad traveled well, and I've taken them to my house. Right now they're resting. I'm sorry about our plans," he added.

He thought Kate looked almost relieved but decided he must have imagined it.

"I don't mind," she said. "Really. If my folks were around and had just come home from overseas, I'd want to spend the first night with them too. We can go to dinner another time."

Aaron crossed the room and linked his hands loosely at Kate's waist. She smiled without meeting his gaze.

"The other couple involved in the house swap won't move out for another month," Aaron said heavily. "Until then, Dad and Mum have asked to stay with me."

"Oh." Kate was quiet for a moment before she smiled. "It's a good thing you were able to do that for them."

Aaron dropped a kiss on her hair and stepped away. "I guess, but I really wanted us to spend time together without any extra pressures."

"It probably won't make any difference," Kate said.

It made more difference than even Aaron had expected. A week later he'd had enough. He hadn't been alone with Kate for more than a few minutes. His mother took her to the mall, talked shopping and child care and whatever else came up. His father dragged her off to show her his favorite garden nursery. When Aaron did get an occasional moment with her, he felt as if she was resisting him.

At the weekend, his sister Phoebe surprised everybody by walking out of her university course and coming home "to think about the future." She landed on Grandma's doorstep and declared her intention to stay.

Aaron felt himself slowly coming unraveled as he faced the prospect of another family member muscling in on his time with Kate.

Somehow he had to get his parents out of his house and back into theirs. Phoebe could move in with them, and he and Kate could return to the plans he had made before these upheavals started. Maybe then she would lose that fidgety, worried look.

Aaron nodded to himself as he stepped out of his truck and wandered into another family get-together, this one at Grandma's home.

First thing tomorrow he would visit Joe and Fiona at his parents' house and see if he could convince them to move into another one until their visit ended.

❦

That plan didn't work out either.

"You must stay as long as you need to, Joe," Aaron said to the middle-aged man the next day. "I know when Dad and Mum understand your situation, they'll agree. I have plenty of room at my house for them."

Joe's anxious face relaxed slightly. "If you're sure, Aaron. I don't want to put you out, but with Fiona feeling the way she does right now, a couple more weeks of rest would be an answer to our prayers."

Aaron shook Joe's hand before he left. "Don't give it another thought. The only thing that matters is that Fiona has every chance to rest and restore her good health."

He was ashamed of the momentary burst of irritation he felt as he left the house and climbed into his truck. Neither Joe nor Fiona could help what had happened.

Forgive me, Lord, he prayed silently, *and please help Fiona recover.*

He had known something was wrong when Joe answered the door. The usually cheerful man had deep lines etched in his cheeks and between his brows. They had barely started talking when Joe confided that Fiona had succumbed to the nervous breakdown that had threatened for months as a result of stress at her work.

Joe had her under the care of a good Ferntree Heights doctor who had recommended that Fiona rest a little longer before facing the trip back to New Zealand.

Aaron banged his hand on the steering wheel. "I'll have to find some other way to be with Kate. I solve problems on the job every day. I'll think of something."

One "something" followed another in an endless line of plans that failed. The trip to Sydney expanded to include his entire family; an attempt to take Kate to dinner failed when his sister informed him she had already planned a family gathering for that evening. Suzie's fourth birthday was a family event where he scarcely said more than two words to Kate.

Soon afterward, Aaron spoke to Kate at work one lunchtime. He pulled her close for a much-needed hug, felt her resistance, and reluctantly released her. Here at the office probably wasn't the right place.

"I have to visit a farm," he said. "It's about a two-hour drive from here into rough country, but the scenery should be beautiful."

He paused, reflecting on what he knew so far of the potential client. "Actually I wouldn't usually take it on, simply because of the distance. The only reason I'm willing to look at it at all is because they've requested wrought-iron work."

He paused to give Kate a hopeful smile. "I thought maybe we could go together. It's during the day, so it will be no different as far as Suzie is concerned. She can stay with Grandma, and we can enjoy some time together, just the two of us."

Kate hesitated. "I guess that would be okay. When would we go?"

Aaron held himself back from rubbing his hands together. Finally, something was going right! "We'll make the trip tomorrow—first thing in the morning."

They started out in thick fog, normal for the beginning of summer. Later it would probably clear into one of the glorious, blue-skied days that seemed to stretch on forever.

Aaron found himself whistling as he drove the truck along the highway. "We have a sealed road for the first half hour," he said, smiling in Kate's direction, "so enjoy it while you can."

"I will," she told him.

She had been silent since getting in the truck, and he

wished he knew what she was thinking.

Aaron slowed for a tight corner and came upon a group of kangaroos about to leap across the road. Fortunately he was far enough back that there was no danger of hitting any of the creatures whose gray fur glistened with the moisture from the fog.

"Oh, look!" Kate exclaimed. "There's a red one!"

Aaron slowed the truck to a crawl as the five kangaroos hopped across the road. They kept pace with the truck on a parallel route beside the road for several seconds before loping off into the bush.

"The mother had a joey in her pouch," Kate exclaimed. "I saw its feet sticking out as she was hopping along."

Aaron nodded, smiling as he increased the speed of the vehicle once more. "It's funny how the baby kangaroos travel upside down a lot of the time. Maybe it's because they can't fit their big feet in!"

Kate laughed. "I guess we'd better look out for other animals too. It wouldn't be the first time I've seen a wombat waddle across the road, and, unfortunately, they aren't as fast as the 'roos, so you have to be twice as careful."

Aaron had often seen the small stout creatures make their homes near camping sites, where they would come out at night and snuffle quietly under cover of darkness.

He took a deep breath of the fresh air filtering in through the vehicle's ventilation system and smiled. The Australian summer Christmas was two weeks away, and, fog or no fog, he was certain he had never seen such a glorious day. As he turned off the road into a thicker, denser fog, he felt as though he and Kate were the only two people in the world.

He glanced at her. "I'm glad we could do this today."

She smiled back. "I am too."

"Tell me what you've been doing over the past few days," Aaron asked. "I've barely had time to talk to you long enough to ask. Have you taken Suzie to the library to sign her up for the special children's program?"

As Kate told him about what she'd been doing, Aaron became aware of the deep impact his family had made on her, not only by their physical presence in her life, but in other ways too.

She had never been part of a family with sisters and brothers, mother and father.

He suddenly realized he had been selfish for wanting to keep her all to himself, but he pushed the thought aside. "I'm glad you get along so well with my family," he said, "but don't let them take over your life, okay? They could easily because they like you so much and want to include you in what they're doing."

"They're all very special," Kate said, her voice becoming wistful. "They've received me with open arms from the beginning. First Marie and Grandma, then your parents and Phoebe."

She sighed. "They have a really strong faith, haven't they?"

Aaron nodded, perturbed by the unhappy cadence of her voice. "I guess they have, but they're just ordinary people like you and me."

She didn't comment.

As they moved farther into the dense bush land, the fog thickened. Outside the truck, fern trees bowed their fronds to the pressure of the mist, while the tall gums stood silently chilled. A peacock gave a lone cry somewhere in the distance. The sound added to the feeling of isolation.

Aaron slowed the truck to a crawl. "I'm starting to wish I'd asked the man for clearer instructions. I didn't expect the fog to stay this long."

Kate agreed. "We could be in for one of those days where the fog lifts at three, only to come down again at five past three for the rest of the day!"

"You could be right." Aaron was still thinking about that possibility when the truck hit a boulder. The vehicle bounced to the left, nose-dived into a slough of swampy mud, and sank to its axles before shuddering to a standstill, engine purring as though nothing adverse had occurred.

The whole thing had happened in seconds, with even the truck's four-wheel drive unable to save them.

"I'd better take a look." He laid a hand on Kate's arm as she reached for the door handle. "Stay here while I check it out. There's no need for both of us to get messed up."

Aaron opened the door and glanced around. The swampy patch extended quite a distance. It was clear this vehicle wouldn't be going anywhere without the aid of a tractor or tow truck.

He had a strong urge to kick the tires!

"I hope our client can help us out," he mumbled as he lowered his booted feet into the mud.

Aaron slogged around to Kate's side, opened the door, and held out his arms. "Turn off the ignition for me, and then I'll carry you to dry ground. We'll have to walk. It can't be too far to Mr. Finn's house."

Kate's hair smelled of wildflowers. He lingered over it a moment before starting the slow move to drier ground.

Mud sucked at his boots from underneath and oozed in from above. The legs of his jeans dragged heavily. He told himself Kate's stiffness in his arms was because of the circumstances. Once on dry ground, they walked the long, rutted road until they came to a mailbox that bore the name "Finn" in washed-out letters.

"This has to be it." He turned to Kate. "How are you holding up?"

She squared her shoulders. "I'm fine. This is a cinch compared to pushing Suzie's stroller up some of those hills in Ferntree Heights."

She glanced down at his muddy legs. "I think you got the worst end of things."

They followed the driveway until they reached a run-down fibro house. Chickens scratched about in the overgrown garden. The home had clearly been well cared for in the past.

As they approached, Aaron saw a figure move in a wicker chair on the verandah. A hand lifted in greeting, and he raised his own to acknowledge it.

"That must be Geordan Finn," he said quietly. "Let's hope he has a tractor."

They climbed the stairs toward the elderly gentleman.

"Hello." Aaron gripped the gnarled hand and smiled. "I'm Aaron Frazer of Frazer's Fencing." He indicated Kate. "And this is Kate Long, my office assistant. You must be Mr. Finn. We have an appointment today to discuss some wrought-iron work."

The pale green eyes examined him slowly. "Didn't you get the second letter telling you we'd changed our minds? No sense putting up a new fence when the son-in-law is going to shift us into some newfangled place in town."

Aaron couldn't believe it. He had driven all the way out here and bogged his truck just to hear that a letter had gone astray! Would anything ever go right for him again?

"I'm sorry," he told Geordan Finn. "I'm afraid we didn't get your second letter."

"I gave it to the wife to post last time our daughter drove her into town. Maybe she forgot." The old man motioned behind him. "I see you walked in. Have you had trouble with your vehicle?"

"We had a slight accident on the way here." Aaron pointed to the road behind them. "Our vehicle is stuck in a marsh some distance back there. Is there any way you could help us get it out? If you have a tractor we could borrow—"

The old man stood slowly, and Aaron saw how frail he was. "Don't keep a tractor nowadays," the man said. "We don't have a telephone either, but there's a two-way radio inside the house. I'll be happy to try our neighbor's place for you. I'm sure he wouldn't mind coming out. Please come in."

While Mr. Finn was trying to call his neighbor, his wife came in from the back of the house where she had been hanging out the wash. She was as frail as her husband. Both were determined to extend hospitality to their unexpected visitors but seemed too tired to do so. After several attempts, Mr. Finn gave up on the two-way radio calls, which for some reason failed to go through.

Aaron thanked them for their kindness and insisted they would be fine waiting beside the truck for a tow vehicle. "I have my cell phone with me. I'll call right now."

He did so while the old couple watched anxiously. After the call, he reassured them that the tow truck driver was familiar with the area and would be there to help them as soon as possible.

He and Kate headed back to the truck.

"I feel sorry for those people," Kate said quietly as they walked the bush track. "I can see they love their home, but I know if they were my parents, I would be concerned about their being way out here on their own, unable to drive, and without a telephone."

Aaron agreed. "I hope they can adjust and enjoy their new surroundings when they move into town."

The tow truck arrived sometime later. When the driver had pulled them from the bog, Aaron turned to Kate before starting back to Ferntree Heights.

"I'm sorry about our day."

Indeed he was sorry for every mislaid plan that had strewn their recent past. If God thought this was a good way to develop his patience, Aaron decided maybe he and God had their wires crossed somewhere. He had never felt less inclined toward patience in his life!

He glanced at Kate again, easing the truck back onto the main road. "If I had known it would work out like this, I wouldn't have suggested this trip."

eleven

Kate had problems of her own. The more time that passed, the less she believed a relationship could ever work out between her and Aaron.

It was hard to trust God with it when she had done that once before and felt abandoned by Him. Each time she felt Aaron trying to draw closer, her fears rose up, and she found herself forcing a distance between them.

She couldn't help comparing herself with Aaron. His faith was so much stronger than hers. She had told herself she could grow to where he was without his needing to know of her struggle. Each day she tried to trust God more, but too many times she felt she was never going to make it.

It only got worse when she met Aaron's parents and Phoebe. They seemed so strong, so yielded to God and full of faith that Kate felt her inadequacies must flash out like a neon sign every time she went near them. They certainly wouldn't want her to be close to Aaron if they realized what she was like.

With these feelings hounding her, Kate planned a barbecue for the family and told Aaron about it.

"We've been going to the activities they've planned, and I thought it was time I did the work. I know they're free from other commitments Saturday," she said, "so the short notice shouldn't be a problem. I've already bought chicken kebabs and green king prawns, as well as a big batch of beef mince to make rissoles."

She smiled and touched his arm, not wanting him to know just how nervous she was. "I hope it's fine with you."

The words of encouragement she had hoped for didn't emerge. Instead Aaron's eyes sparked with irritation.

"Did you need to plan this?" He ran a hand impatiently through his hair. "We spend most of our free time with them already. We could have done something together tomorrow—seen a movie or gone on that bush walk you suggested ages ago. I know Grandma would take care of Suzie for a couple of hours."

Kate was hurt. She had thought Aaron would be pleased. "I've already organized it. I can't cancel at the last minute."

He searched her face, and she felt herself grow hot at his lengthy perusal.

"All right," he said, frowning. "I guess if it's planned, there's nothing we can do about it."

"I'm sorry," she said. "I should have talked to you before I made any firm plans."

It was an olive branch, and she was glad when his expression cleared and he smiled.

"I should have told you what I had in mind too," he admitted. "In the future we'll both talk to each other about our plans."

She returned his smile, aching a little because she wasn't at all certain they would have any future plans to make. "Okay."

❦

On the surface the barbecue was a success. The salads were colorful and inviting, the meats cooked to perfection. Everyone praised Kate's culinary efforts, the day remained clear and cloudless, and the family stayed well into the afternoon to chat over coffee and apple pie.

Kate's attention was caught when Aaron's grandmother turned to his mother.

"Have you worked out your schedule yet, Lorraine?" Grandma Bennet asked.

"Yes, I was able to take over the Help for the Disheartened program again," the younger woman told her. "There's such a strong need for people who have lost their way, and we're not going to find those folks sitting in our churches on Sundays. Jesus said to go out into the highways and byways. That's what I plan to do."

"Let me know if I can help in any way," Grandma Bennet said.

She turned to Kate. "Lorraine set this group up several years ago, and it's been going strong ever since. I'm sure she was missed while she was in New Zealand."

Lorraine glanced at her husband. "Hugh finds some time to help, too, when he isn't delivering meals to the elderly on the church roster program. He filled that gap almost as soon as we got home. He's also helping with painting the new fence around the children's outdoor play area at the church."

She turned to Kate. "Did you know Aaron donated the materials and supervised the building?"

Kate shook her head.

"No," she said quietly, "I didn't know that."

Aaron's parents were the first to leave. Hugh shook hands with Kate while Lorraine smiled in that gentle way she had. "Thank you, Dear," she said. "We've had a lovely day."

Kate leaned forward to receive her kiss on the cheek, but her heart was heavy. "It was my pleasure."

Grandma went upstairs to rest before dinner, and Phoebe asked if she could take Suzie downtown to the ice cream shop. That left Aaron and Kate by themselves.

Kate picked up the few items that hadn't been washed yet. The day might have been a success for the others, but for her it had been a dismal failure. If she had set out deliberately to prove how hopeless she was, she thought she couldn't have done a better job.

"I think we need to talk," Aaron said into the silence.

He sounded serious. Kate would have preferred to leave it until some other time when she didn't feel quite so downtrodden, but she tossed the garbage into a bag and turned to face him. "What about?"

He ran a hand over his face. "About us, for one thing. Is there a problem you're not telling me about? Don't you want to spend time with me?"

"I—of course I do." Kate's eyebrows rose. "What do you mean by that question?"

He shrugged his shoulders. "You've barely looked at me since I arrived. I know I'm not imagining that. Are you trying to find a way out, Kate?"

Was she?

Kate's heart plummeted at the thought.

"No! I—"

She didn't know what she wanted.

God, why aren't You here to help me when I need You?

She shifted her gaze to the top button of Aaron's shirt. "I'm sorry if I ignored you. I was trying to be a good hostess to your family."

Aaron shook his head and pushed his hands deep into his back pockets. "They can look after themselves. There are other priorities for the two of us now. Don't you remember how much we both felt the need to spend time together? Our relationship is still new. I want to make it strong, and I think we need some time alone to do that."

Kate drew a deep breath. "I need time to get to know your family, as well as you."

"You've spent a lot of time at family gatherings lately," Aaron pointed out.

"I know." She raised her chin. "This was the first time I had done something for them, and I'd hoped you would support me in it."

He took her hands in his. "I'm sorry. I do admire you for all the hard work you put into making today special, and maybe after this we can spend some time together—just us."

❦

Kate's deepest fear was that she would never be worthy of Aaron. David had quickly grown tired of her and even resented being married to her. She had a dreadful suspicion that if he hadn't died that night, she may not have been able to salvage her marriage.

The more she saw of Aaron's family, the more convinced she became that she would never measure up. When Grandma Bennet and Phoebe went to a flower show, she decided to visit Marie. Perhaps some time with her friend would remind her that not all of Aaron's family members were in perfect control of their lives!

"It's kind of lonely over at Grandma's," Kate said when she arrived.

Marie smiled as she directed Suzie to where the children were playing. Then she turned back to Kate.

"You don't need to tell me anything about loneliness," Marie said. "I've suffered it for months now, remember. When do Grandma and Phoebe return from the garden show?"

Kate took the chair Marie indicated at the kitchen table.

"Tomorrow evening. I worry about them a little, being over there in Adelaide. It's so far away if anything happens."

"Phoebe is sensible—she would know what to do," Marie said. "Besides, God will take good care of them." Suddenly a bright smile lit her face.

"I have something to tell you." Her voice rose with excitement. "Jeremy's coming home early. He managed to get in phone contact last week, and we talked." She laughed. "He wanted to cut his trip short, so he's worked really hard to shave some time off. We're still not sure exactly when he'll get a flight back into the country, but at least we know it won't be too long before we see him. We'll be a whole family again."

Kate went over to Marie and hugged her. "That's wonderful news."

Marie nodded. "You know, when I thought about it, I realized I'd felt threatened by Jeremy's absence. Sometimes we let our imagination run amok. I allowed myself to get focused on me. What would happen to me if Jeremy didn't want to come back? How would I cope? When I realized the way my thoughts were going, I went to the Lord and asked for forgiveness. The very next day Jeremy phoned to say he wanted to come home."

"Maybe he'll be home in time for Christmas," Kate offered, even as her heart sank at this final proof of her own shortcomings.

Marie had been the one member of Aaron's family who had shown some vulnerability. Kate had clung to that knowledge like a lifeline. She was pleased that Marie had solved her problems—she truly was—but she also felt hurt to discover her friend was beyond her spiritual reach too.

"You mentioned grocery shopping when we talked on the phone," Marie said with a smile. "Why don't you leave Suzie with me while you take care of it and give yourself a break for a few hours?"

"Thanks." Kate's heart was heavy, but she returned the smile. Time alone was probably exactly what she needed right now. "I think I'll take you up on that."

Kate stayed awhile longer as Marie told her about her plans for the future. Then she told Suzie she would be back later and left. She changed her mind about the shopping and instead drove out to a favorite spot where she could see the mountains and valleys on every side.

Today she couldn't appreciate the beauty of the blue green horizon.

The facts were simple. She wasn't good enough for Aaron. She never had been, and she never would be. He would soon tire of her when he realized that, and she would much rather walk away before that happened. The alternative would be too painful to bear.

Kate stood there for a long time, thinking about it all. When she finally turned back toward her car, the sun lay low in the sky, and the evening mist had rolled in.

She set her shoulders and returned to Ferntree Heights for the last time.

❦

Kate had never written a more difficult letter. She threw

away dozens of drafts before she finally settled on a brief statement of why their relationship must end.

Every time she allowed herself to think about Aaron, she felt as though her heart were being torn in two. It hurt more than anything she had felt before, even losing David. She couldn't do anything to ease the pain. The time had come to make a decision, and she had made it.

God hadn't been there to show her the way, so she had done her best on her own.

Kate flushed at her thoughts. She knew God had been there; she just hadn't been able to yield to Him—

"No," she whispered fiercely. "I am not going to think about that now. The decision is made, and there's no going back."

Finished at last, she wrote two more letters, one to Grandma Bennet and one to Marie, thanking each of them for all they had given into her life. Then she moved quietly about the house and packed things to go in the car first thing tomorrow. When she finally fell into bed, her head ached from wrestling with her doubts; her throat ached from tears held back. A part of her wanted to go to Aaron in the hope that he would try to convince her to stay. She fought within herself for the strength to stand firm on her decision.

She rose at first light. The crimson sky reflected the turbulence of her mood. The few hours of fitful sleep had done little to settle her uneasy state of mind. Tension pulled the muscles of her neck and pinched a line of pain between her eyes.

She only got the car half loaded before Suzie woke. The struggle to tie everything onto the roof rack took time.

Even when she had finished the job, Kate wasn't entirely happy with the placement of the load, but it would have to do. She knew the moment her daughter caught sight of the boxes, the questions would start, so she led her quietly into the kitchen and sat her down at the table. "Let me explain what's happening."

Suzie's trusting eyes looked up into hers. A fierce guilt stabbed through Kate as she admitted that her daughter would be uprooted for the second time in her four-year-old life because of this choice.

"I know what I plan to tell you will be a surprise," she began gently, "and at first you might not like the idea, but this is what we're going to do."

Her daughter waited silently, so she plowed on.

"Mama has been very happy here with Grandma Bennet and everyone, but now it's time to leave." She took Suzie's hands in hers and gave them a squeeze. "We're going to a new town where I'll find a good job, and we'll get ourselves a nice place to stay. I have some money saved up to help us."

"I don't want to go," Suzie said, her little face drooping with sadness.

Kate turned away from the sight of her daughter's brimming eyes and quivering lower lip. She drew in her breath before she turned back to take Suzie into her arms.

"I'm sorry, Sweetheart," she said, "but you don't have a choice. This is what Mama has decided is best for us."

Kate's heart ached. Tears rose to her eyes, and she fought to keep them in. She wanted to bury her face in her daughter's hair and weep.

Suzie didn't yell or scream or throw a tantrum. She

sobbed. All Kate's efforts to soothe her failed. In the end she left her to cry on the sofa while she rushed to get the rest of the boxes into the car. Maybe once they got on the road, Suzie would settle down. If she kept this up much longer, she would make herself sick.

She still needed to deliver the farewell letter to the warehouse suite. She knew Aaron planned to go straight to a job on the northern edge of town and stay there until at least midmorning, so they weren't likely to meet.

She placed the letters to Grandma and Marie against the cold teapot on the kitchen table beside her house key, lifted Suzie from the sofa, and locked the front door after them.

With her daughter strapped into her seat beside the roof-high pile of belongings, Kate drove directly to the warehouse. The early hour meant nobody would notice her. She spent long moments wandering back and forth among the fencing supplies as she wrestled with her memories, her convictions, and her heart. She had just placed the letter and keys on the desk when Marie stepped over the threshold.

"What's going on, Kate? Suzie's out there in the car looking like her best friend just died, and you're packed up to the roof. Where are you going? What's happened?"

Kate swallowed. "Marie, I didn't expect to see you this morning." For a moment she couldn't go on. The sudden meeting left her emotionally unprepared. She took a deep breath and willed her lips not to tremble. "I'm leaving town. Things haven't worked out as I'd hoped they would, and it's time for me to go. I left you a letter back at Grandma's, but now that you're here, I'll say it in person. Thank you for being my friend."

Marie's hands went to her hips in that no-nonsense way

she had. "Will you please tell me what this is all about? Where do you plan to go?"

Kate pressed her lips together and then inhaled sharply before explaining why she couldn't tell her.

A childish voice spoke up first. "We're going to Queensland."

Kate whirled. "Suzie, why are you out here?"

The little girl scurried over and clung to her mother's leg. "I wanted to see Aaron."

"He's not here, Honey. Now, please, get back in the car. I'll be there in a minute."

"I don't want to go. I want to see Aaron," Suzie repeated.

Suzie's lip trembled again, and Kate heard herself speak more sternly than she should have.

"Go back to the car. Now."

Suzie reluctantly peeled herself from Kate's leg and went outside, her small shoulders stiff with hurt.

Kate watched until her daughter climbed back into the car and then turned to Marie. "I have to go. Please don't make it any harder than it already is, and I must ask you not to tell Aaron our plans. A clean break will be better for all of us."

Marie shook her head. "I'm sorry, Kate, but I can't agree to do that. I believe with all my heart that this is a mistake. Won't you sit down with me and talk about it? Maybe we can sort it out together."

Kate shook her head. "No. I'm sorry." The tears she'd fought down since the night before filled her eyes. "It would be better if Aaron didn't follow us, so I'm asking you again to let us go."

Marie remained silent. Kate searched her face for a long

moment and, finding no response, quickly went to the car.

She strapped Suzie in securely while Marie watched. Then she met Marie's glance as she climbed behind the wheel. "You know what I'm asking of you, Marie. I hope you'll respect my wishes."

She drove away without looking back, unsure of what Marie would do.

After the first few kilometers, Suzie quieted. A glance in the rearview mirror showed that her daughter was sleeping. All the crying had exhausted her. As she mentally mapped out the route she would take to Queensland, Kate tried to pray, but the words wouldn't form.

She felt distanced from the Lord, and then she remembered something her grandmother used to say.

If you feel as though God is a long way from you, guess which one of you moved?

"I'm doing the right thing," she said out loud. The words echoed hollowly around the interior of the car.

"Lord," Kate prayed quietly, "I do believe You'll never leave us or forsake us. I'm doing my best to be a strong Christian, and I know I've grown, but I still can't trust You with my future."

It made her heart ache to say it, but she went on. "I'm not sorry I had the chance to know Aaron and to see his faith in You. I'd like to have the same kind of faith, and maybe one day I will, but I have to accept that I'm not the right person to be part of his life."

She had thought the prayer might help, but the sense of peace Kate had hoped for eluded her as she continued the trip. Indeed, the farther she traveled, the more she wanted to turn back. When she glanced at her watch, it surprised her to realize that less than thirty minutes had passed since she left.

Kate began to feel more and more agitated. She had such a deep sense that she had done the wrong thing that she couldn't ignore it a moment longer.

Outside one of the small townships, she forced herself to face her thoughts. She realized she had allowed her fears to overrule her good sense and that it wasn't up to her to decide whether or not she was "good enough" for Aaron.

Jesus had loved her enough to lay His life down for her. He hadn't demanded that she achieve anything before He gave her that gift.

Everyone fell short of the glory of God. No one could earn His great love by their own efforts. He chose to love them, just as He wanted them to choose to trust Him—with everything.

Kate's hands shook as her thoughts whirled around in her head. She didn't trust herself to drive while she felt like this. She put on the blinker and tried to pull the little car to the side of the road.

In her agitation, she made the turn too quickly. In the seconds that followed, she felt the load on the roof racks shift. A suitcase thudded onto the hood of the car. She braked sharply and veered, clipping it as it fell to the ground.

The sound of shattering glass testified to a broken headlight, and she brought the car to a standstill on the shoulder of the road. Kate stared through the windshield, trembling.

The noise awakened Suzie. "Mama? What happened? Did we bump?"

Kate shut her lips against a bubble of hysterical laughter. "Yes, Darling, we did. Stay here while I see what's broken."

She climbed out of the car and walked around the front. Her legs shook more than she cared to admit as she surveyed the situation. The load on the roof racks had skewed to one side. One headlight was smashed, and a large crumple mark decorated the fender. Kate picked up the mangled suitcase and brushed some of the dust from it. Miraculously the clothes had stayed inside, although what state they would be in remained to be seen.

"Just goes to show how much of a pounding a good suitcase can take," she muttered in a feeble attempt at humor.

She looked back at the road again, first ahead, then behind. "Okay, Lord. I know I've been stubborn, and I know it's taken me far too long, but I want to hand it all over to You. What do I do now?"

Aaron pulled off his protective gloves as his sister's white Holden station wagon swerved to a standstill beside his truck.

"I'll be back in a minute, Shane. You can check those sheets of corrugated iron while you wait. It looks like we're short."

He strode toward Marie as she jumped from the car.

He searched her face. "What's wrong?"

"Something terrible—"

Marie threw herself into his arms.

His heart pounded as the questions rose in his mind.

She drew back to look at him.

"Kate has just left town," she said quickly. "I tried to stop her, but she wouldn't listen to me."

"What do you mean—she's left town? Is Suzie ill? Has something happened to Grandma?"

"No." Marie shook her head. "Kate has packed everything into her car and left for good."

Aaron frowned, a deep unease gnawing at him. "Kate wouldn't pack up and leave town without even speaking to me first. She wouldn't turn her back on me, on us. You have to be mistaken."

"I'm sorry, Aaron, but I'm not," Marie said.

He listened, groaning inwardly, as she explained how she had discovered Kate at the warehouse.

"It's a miracle I even saw her," Marie said. "Sam Jones gave me a check to pass on to you, and I decided I'd drive it over and push it under the door of your suite, before I forgot about it. I left Rowan in charge in case the other two children woke, and then I drove over. That's when I saw Kate."

"What did she say? How did she seem?" Aaron ran a hand through his hair. "I have to bring her back, Marie, so tell me quickly. I need to get on the road."

Once Marie had told him everything she could, she handed him a plain white envelope. "She left this for you at the warehouse. I thought it might shed some light on things."

Aaron's fingers felt like blocks of wood as he fumbled to break the seal. He drew out the single sheet and focused on Kate's neat print.

Dear Aaron,

By the time you open this, I'll already be on my way to a new life.

I apologize for leaving my job without giving proper notice. I know you'll be able to find someone else, but maybe Marie could help you out while you search.

I'm sorry things didn't work out between us, but I have come to realize that our relationship wasn't meant to be. One day you'll find a woman who will be right for you, somebody who can give you all the good things you deserve in a wife.

Suzie and I will miss you and always remember you with love.

Sincerely,
Kate

He crumpled the letter in his fist and turned back to Marie. "This is my fault. If I hadn't been so impatient and pushed her when she wasn't ready, this could have been avoided. She's the one for me and as worthy of my love as any other person. Somehow I've allowed her to believe otherwise."

Marie's face reflected her concern. "What will you do?"

"I have to find her," Aaron said.

"I'll pray for the Lord to help you," Marie promised.

"Thanks, Sis."

Aaron hugged his sister and headed straight for the truck, thankful that Shane had all the materials for this job on the back of his Ford Ute. Kate had to be stopped before she got so far away that he couldn't track her. He sprang into the driver's seat and gunned the engine, the fear of losing her coursing through him.

In seconds he discovered he had a flat tire. Stifling his frustration, he jumped out and crossed to where Marie was about to climb into her station wagon. "I must have hit a nail or something. Can I borrow your car?"

She passed him the keys and stepped out of the way.

"Go quickly, Aaron. Find her."

He waved Shane over. "Could you take care of things? Marie will explain."

"Sure, Boss."

"Thanks." Aaron turned toward Marie's car. Somehow the Lord would have to keep Kate where he could find her, despite the lost time. Maybe she would stop somewhere to buy food for Suzie.

Marie had said Kate intended to go to Queensland, so she would most likely head down the mountains and toward Sydney.

Irritated at the slow pace forced on him by the winding road, he tried to fathom why Kate had left.

What had he done or not done to bring her to a place where she felt their relationship could not succeed? A feeling of guilt pierced him. He had been impatient and demanded too much, too soon.

Aaron spotted an orange car on the road ahead and caught his breath, his heart pounding in his ears. He stepped on the gas pedal and closed the gap.

It wasn't Kate.

He dropped back to a safer speed.

Where is she, Lord? Am I even on the right road?

Doubts crowded in and for a moment threatened to overwhelm him. How could he hope to find her? She could be anywhere.

"She's on this road, and I will catch up with her and convince her to come back home." Aaron clenched his jaw. "The Lord is in control of this situation. He won't let me lose Kate."

A line from Kate's letter flashed through his mind. *One*

day you'll find a woman who will be right for you. It went on to say something about what he deserved in a wife.

His heart squeezed tight. Had he failed to esteem her to such a degree? The opposite was true. Any man would be privileged to share his life with a woman who so obviously loved God and wanted to serve Him with all her heart.

"Ah, Kate. Why did you run away?"

twelve

"Kate! Are you all right?"

Aaron's voice startled Kate from trying to reposition the load on top of her car.

She turned, inhaling sharply as she saw Aaron's face only a few meters away. "How did you find me?"

"Marie told me." Aaron shook his head. "That's not important. Are you hurt? What happened here?"

"I'm fine." She glanced at the damaged car and back to him. "I had a little accident when I pulled off the side of the road."

Aaron approached her slowly, as though he feared she would jump in her car and drive off if he moved any faster.

Kate's heart ached.

For him, for her, for the hurt she saw in his expression and felt in her own heart.

"Why did you run, Kate?" His voice was husky. "Did you think I would let you leave without finding out how I drove you away?"

Her hands fell slowly to her sides. She stepped further away from the vehicle, searching for the right words to explain what she had done and why she'd stopped.

Help me, Lord. It's in Your hands.

"At the time I thought it was best."

Aaron took a step closer. "There are things we need to say to each other. Come back to town."

He put his hand on her arm, not caressing, not enveloping. Just resting.

Waiting.

Asking silently.

She looked at him. "I never wanted to hurt you."

His hand tightened. "I'm glad of that."

She wiped her hand across her face and drew a deep breath. "I pulled over because I meant to come back to talk to you. I hope it's not too late."

"It's never too late."

The back door of the Volkswagen swung open. Suzie appeared, a curious look on her face. "Why is Aaron here, Mama?"

Aaron bent down to speak to the little girl. "Would you like to ride back to town with me, Suzie? Your mother and I need to talk."

Before Kate could object, Suzie agreed and trotted off to climb into Marie's station wagon.

"Is your car okay, Kate?" Aaron asked.

Kate followed as he walked to the front of the Volkswagen. "A suitcase came off the roof racks and hit the hood," she explained. "I knew the load wasn't secure enough when I tied it on, but I guess I wasn't thinking straight. I'm just glad I didn't hurt anyone. It smashed the headlight and dented a fender. I should still be able to drive the car though."

Aaron glanced at her from head to foot. "That suitcase could have gone through the windshield and killed you."

She shook her head, unable to stop the feeling of love that surged through her at his concern. "I was almost at a standstill when it happened."

"I'm glad you're okay." He blew out a breath and turned back to inspect the front of the car. "Not a pretty picture, but safe to drive, as you said. I'll go first, you follow. If you have any problems, flash your lights, and I'll pull over." For the first time since he arrived, he attempted a smile. "Make that—flash your light."

❦

Aaron glanced in the rearview mirror again. Now that he had Kate back, he didn't plan to lose sight of her for a second. If he could have sorted things out on the side of the road back there, he would have, but some things required time and the right setting.

He wanted to build a new life with Kate, raise Suzie together, grow in faith as a couple, and maybe add some more children somewhere down the line.

What do I do, Lord? How do I tell Kate what is on my heart? I've pushed her too hard once already and suffered the results. I don't want to make the same mistake again. Yet I can't let her walk out of my life without making it clear how much I want her to stay.

He picked up his cell phone and caught Suzie's glance in the rearview mirror. "Would you like to visit at Marie's house, while I take your mother somewhere to talk?"

Her wide eyes met his with absolute trust. "Okay."

He smiled and received the reward of her warm smile in return. "Good girl."

Kate hugged his sister briefly in silence and waited on the footpath as Marie took Suzie inside. Aaron gave a prayer of thanks when he saw the crew cab in the driveway, tires intact.

Praying for God's help and a clear mind, he ushered

Kate into the vehicle. "We can get your car later."

Her silence during the short drive made it impossible for him to gauge her feelings. When they arrived, he turned to her as she released her seat belt. "Dad and Mum are out of town today, so we can talk in private here."

Now that he wasn't driving, he could see that she was nervous and pale. Her hands shook slightly as she reached for the door handle.

Help me, Lord. If I must still wait, give me the strength to do it.

Aaron led Kate to a seat on the front porch and sat down beside her. He almost said something about the weather but checked himself.

Nerves.

Kate looked at him.

"From the beginning I've believed we were meant to be together," he said, "but I know you've had your doubts. What can I say to help you believe our relationship can work?"

She lowered her eyes. "You don't have to say anything. I've been very foolish. Just when I was starting to realize how much the Lord loves me and cares about every part of my life, I fell back into doubt and fear again, and I was so stubborn. I knew I needed to surrender my life, but where you were concerned, I was afraid to trust Him."

Hope rose in Aaron's heart. "And now?"

She turned clear blue gray eyes on his face. "I should never have left in the way I did. All of this could have been avoided if I'd trusted Him."

Aaron lifted her chin with one finger. The scent of wild-flowers drifted from her skin, drawing him closer.

"I'm to blame too," he admitted. "You told me you needed

time." He grimaced. "I tried to be patient, but I haven't had a lot of practice at being a patient man. After your illness, I sort of snapped. I wanted you in my life where I could be near you all the time. I set out to win you, and when you showed you had doubts, I ignored them most of the time."

Kate touched Aaron's face with her hand. "I guess we've both made mistakes. But I know the Lord has been with me through the difficulties and the triumphs, and He's been there for you too. I'm sorry I took matters into my own hands and didn't trust Him to lead me. It's a mistake I don't ever want to repeat."

She took a deep breath and met Aaron's warm brown gaze. "I was afraid I would never be good enough for you. Everyone in your family is so committed to the Lord and so active in ministry that I thought I could never live up to them or to you."

Aaron moved toward her, but she held up her hand. If he touched her now, she would forget everything, and she needed all her concentration to share the things that lay hidden in her heart. "I thought I would be holding you back if I stayed with you, but I can see I was wrong. I believe the Lord brought us together and that He'll bless us as we follow Him."

It wasn't easy to bare her heart to Aaron this way. Kate held her breath as she waited for his response and prayed that she would have the strength to hold her head up if he rejected her.

"I want you in my life, Kate." Aaron leaned closer until Kate could smell the scent of eucalyptus leaves and bush land on his shirt.

"You in no way fall short of what I've hoped for in a

woman." He lowered his voice and looked deep into her eyes. "In a wife."

The impact of his words brought tears to her eyes. In her most secret heart, Kate had imagined what this moment would be like, how it would feel to hear him speak of a lifetime union before God.

For a long moment they looked into each other's eyes, and she couldn't help but let him see the depth of her love for him. His face softened, and his own gaze warmed in response.

Moved almost beyond words, she closed her eyes before she spoke. "I've longed to hear you say that."

He shook his head. "There are things I want to be sure you understand about me."

His voice held a thread of huskiness.

She saw such vulnerability in his face that her heart squeezed painfully. "What things?"

He stroked a finger absently across the back of her left hand. "I'm not so wonderful, Kate. I have fears, just as much as anybody does. You know I've been impatient, time and again, and I probably will be in the future too."

He looked down at her fingers, and she held her breath. She sensed he had something important to say. When he looked up again, she allowed herself to listen with her heart as well as her head.

"When you came along, I wanted everything at once." Aaron gave a lopsided smile that brought out the dimple in his cheek.

"I can think of a dozen times where I failed to look to the Lord for guidance in our relationship." Aaron released his grip on her hands and stood up.

She rose with him and faced him as he raised his arms and let them drop against his sides.

He grimaced. "All I wanted was to tie you to me, any way I could. I didn't give enough consideration to how my actions would affect you." He pushed his hands into the pockets of his jeans. "I never wanted to drive you away from me, but I did. Now you're back, and I'm telling you my weaknesses so you know who I really am. I'm just an ordinary man who faces the same battles we all do, who sometimes fails and often has to go back to the Lord to ask for forgiveness and the chance to start over again."

Kate shook her head as a feeling of love rushed through her. Aaron stood silently before her. It was so easy to see now that neither of them was perfect, but they were both forgiven and loved by God.

Her throat tightened with the love that she had held in check for so long. She knew that once she released it, there would be no going back.

"Aaron, I—" she said, taking a step toward him. "I shouldn't have held off on trusting the Lord about you the way I did."

She raised a hand to stroke his face. Her fingers trembled as he leaned into her touch.

"I hadn't realized things were difficult for you too," she admitted. "When I started to think about our relationship, a part of me shied away from pursuing it in case it failed somehow and I got hurt.

"Later I worried you'd be hurt, but by then I couldn't bear to be parted from you. Maybe in the end I looked for a way out so I could blame the failure on something I had chosen myself."

She closed her eyes as he raised his hands to her shoulders. When she opened them again, she felt the force of deep love shining from his eyes.

"I do want this relationship, Aaron. I want it to work and for us to be together, if that's still possible."

He caressed her shoulders with his hands. "It is still possible, if you can understand that it's not about worthiness or how far along you think you are in your faith. The Lord loves you just as you are. He sees inside your heart and knows your faith and commitment to Him."

When he lifted one of his hands to stroke her chin, she held her breath.

He lowered his face a little closer. "I love you," he said simply. "I don't expect you to be perfect. You're all I want, just as you are. The two of us will grow together, and it won't be about who has the stronger faith or the most commitment to the Lord or anything else like that."

His final words came out on a soft breath of sound. "We'll be together, and we'll grow in God together. That's all I ask for."

He paused and looked deeply into her eyes. "I think you know what I plan to ask you, Kate, but first I want to show you something. Wait right here. I'll only be a minute."

Aaron returned to her with something wrapped in a piece of old cloth. Kate looked at his face and back down to the large, oval-shaped object as he drew the cloth away to reveal a picture frame.

Kate gasped. "It's beautiful!"

He placed the frame in her hands. "I started to carve this months ago, soon after I realized how much you meant to me, how much I wanted us to be together."

She stared at the beautiful frame. An intricate design of wildflowers, gardenias, lilacs, and violets covered the oval shape. Fern tree fronds leaped to life while rhododendron nestled beside tiny star-shaped wildflowers. He had carved the flowers of her favorite scents, as well as those found around the region. "This is the most beautiful piece of carving I've ever seen. It must have taken so much work."

He laughed softly. "I guess you'd call it a labor of love. When things were difficult, I would work on the carving and pray."

Kate smoothed her fingers over the contours of the wood. "It would look just right above the mantle in the center of your living room."

His expression showed he understood her meaning. The gift belonged to her, after all.

"Yes, I think it would too," he agreed.

She touched the carving again. "It's a big frame. Large enough for—"

He removed it gently from her hands and set it down beside them. "I plan to fill it with a family."

She caught her breath. "You do?"

He smiled and took her into his arms. "I want to spend my life with you, Kate. It's all I long for."

The last of her fears dissolved in the warmth of his love. She raised her face to his, so close. "Are you sure?"

"I am very sure." He pulled her close.

"I love you, Kate," he told her, "with all my heart, with my whole being. You are beautiful." He punctuated the statement with a kiss on her nose. "Talented." He kissed her again. "Generous, sweet-natured, wise, and kind."

He enclosed both her hands in one of his own. "When

you walk into a room, I feel happy just to see you there. When you smile, I can't help smiling back."

She looked down and then lifted her eyes to meet his.

"I–I feel that way too." Her heart was beating rapidly.

"I've never known anyone like you," she admitted. "When we first met, I felt drawn to you in a way I'd never felt before. As I got to know you, I came to respect you and admire your attitudes and the way you lived your life.

"It wasn't long before I realized you were someone I would enjoy knowing better." She shook her head. "Oh, I fought it! I ran scared. I even ran away, but I always wanted your love."

She sighed. "I'm tired of running."

It seemed to be the signal he had waited for. He drew her close.

"Marry me," he said. "Let me love you for the rest of our lives."

Her heart soared with tender feeling. "Yes, I'll marry you."

For one long moment he searched deep in her eyes. She could feel him reach right down into the depths of her heart, and she waited, openly trusting, secure in his love.

Then he drew her close and kissed her. "How soon will you marry me?"

She laughed and drew back a little to give him a teasing glance. "You don't plan to get impatient again, do you?"

For a moment he looked so taken aback that she found it hard to keep a straight face.

"I thought, oh, maybe, well. . ." She trailed off but gave up when he looked so agonized. "How about as soon as we can get things organized?"

He lifted her into his arms and swung her around until

she became dizzy and dissolved into giggles.

"Do I take that as your stamp of approval?" she asked, catching her breath.

"Yes, you do." He lowered her to her feet. "It's a good thing you've spent time with my family. You know exactly what you're getting into, so there'll be no excuses when you find yourself tied to the whole lot of us."

She laughed and touched his arm. "I was intimidated by them, I admit, but not anymore. They're God's creation, just as you and I are, and I already love them."

He drew her hand into his. "They love you too." He paused to look deeply into her eyes again. "Just not the same way I do."

He tugged her hand, and they sank down onto the seat on the porch.

"You know I already love Suzie as if she were my own child," Aaron told her. "I'll do everything I can to be a good father to her."

Kate's eyes misted. "You'll be a wonderful father, and it will be no struggle. Suzie already loves you. I think she'll be thrilled when we tell her our news."

Aaron toyed with her hair for a moment until she stilled his hand.

"I can tell you want to say something," she said. "What is it?"

"How do you feel about having other children?" he asked thoughtfully.

She blinked. "Oh. I'd like to have more children, if you would."

He laughed and released her.

"I would." He stood to his feet. "One more thing."

This time, as he entered the house, she felt only happiness. A burden had lifted from her heart. Inside she had a calm and peace that came from knowing the Lord didn't see her as a failure, but a creature able to grow in the perfect timing He had laid out for her.

Aaron loved her, their relationship stood on the threshold of a bright and beautiful new beginning, and she couldn't imagine adding more joy to what already flowed from her heart.

Then Aaron came back, holding a ring in his hand.

That's when she realized that joy could be like an ever-flowing river that poured out in torrents and never ran dry. "Oh, Aaron."

He sat beside her and lifted her left hand. "I love you, Kate." He slipped the ring onto her finger and raised her hand to his lips.

She slowly lowered her hand. The solitaire diamond sparkled in a setting of white gold. Kate had thought she couldn't be happier, but she was wrong. Her heart felt as though it would burst. "I don't know what to say, how to thank you—"

He touched her cheek. "You don't have to say anything. The look in your eyes tells me what I want to know."

Kate allowed herself to relax into Aaron's strong embrace, content and secure in the knowledge of his love.

Thank You, Lord, for bringing me to this man and him to me.

"Do you know what I'm thinking?" Aaron whispered.

She shook her head slightly. "No, what?"

He smiled gently. "I'm thinking there's a time for everything under heaven and that now is our time."

Kate thought about it. She had read those verses in the Bible many times and could identify with much of their content. She had seen loss and death, had been planted and uprooted again. Hurt and healing had both come her way, along with tears and laughter.

She had warred within herself, but now she had found her place of peace. She smiled. "Yes, now is our time."

A Letter To Our Readers

Dear Reader:

In order that we might better contribute to your reading enjoyment, we would appreciate your taking a few minutes to respond to the following questions. We welcome your comments and read each form and letter we receive. When completed, please return to the following:

Rebecca Germany, Fiction Editor
Heartsong Presents
PO Box 719
Uhrichsville, Ohio 44683

1. Did you enjoy reading *Good Things Come* by Jennifer Ann Ryan?

   ❑ Very much! I would like to see more books by this author!

   ❑ Moderately. I would have enjoyed it more if

   ____

   ____

2. Are you a member of **Heartsong Presents**? Yes ❑ No ❑
   If no, where did you purchase this book?______________

   ____

3. How would you rate, on a scale from 1 (poor) to 5 (superior), the cover design?______________________________

4. On a scale from 1 (poor) to 10 (superior), please rate the following elements.

   _____ Heroine _____ Plot

   _____ Hero _____ Inspirational theme

   _____ Setting _____ Secondary characters

5. These characters were special because____________________

6. How has this book inspired your life?____________________

7. What settings would you like to see covered in future **Heartsong Presents** books?____________________

8. What are some inspirational themes you would like to see treated in future books?____________________

9. Would you be interested in reading other **Heartsong Presents** titles? Yes ❑ No ❑

10. Please check your age range:

❑ Under 18 ❑ 18-24 ❑ 25-34
❑ 35-45 ❑ 46-55 ❑ Over 55

Name ____________________

Occupation ____________________

Address ____________________

City __________ State __________ Zip __________

Email ____________________